## "Who was I to

Joe made himself n
each other a few t~~~~

"You mean dated?"

"Yeah."

A dozen emotions darted across her face in the span of a couple of seconds. "How long?"

"Five months."

Her eyes flickered with surprise. "That long?"

He nodded and she processed that information quietly, but he could see her doing the math. Five months together meant more than just holding hands while walking or a goodnight kiss at the door.

He turned back to his food, aware that he had to keep up his strength, which had already been compromised by the bullet wound. But he couldn't help but wonder if he'd ever have enough strength to deal with many more nights alone with Jane Doe.

# PAULA GRAVES

# COWBOY ALIBI

HARLEQUIN®

TORONTO • NEW YORK • LONDON
AMSTERDAM • PARIS • SYDNEY • HAMBURG
STOCKHOLM • ATHENS • TOKYO • MILAN • MADRID
PRAGUE • WARSAW • BUDAPEST • AUCKLAND

For Jenn, Cissy and Emily, who make wonderful
sounding boards and wonderful friends.

ISBN-13: 978-0-373-69355-9
ISBN-10:  0-373-69355-9

COWBOY ALIBI

# ABOUT THE AUTHOR

Alabama native Paula Graves wrote her first book, a mystery starring herself and her neighborhood friends, at the age of six. A voracious reader, Paula loves books that pair tantalizing mystery with compelling romance. When she's not reading or writing, she works as a creative director for a Birmingham advertising agency and spends time with her family and friends. She is a member of Southern Magic Romance Writers, Heart of Dixie Romance Writers and Romance Writers of America.

Paula invites readers to visit her Web site, www.paulagraves.com.

## Books by Paula Graves

HARLEQUIN INTRIGUE

# CAST OF CHARACTERS

*Jane Doe*—The waitress has no memory of her former life. All she knows is that someone is willing to kill to get to her.

*Joe Garrison*—The embittered Wyoming cop believes Jane was complicit in his brother Tommy's murder. But when someone comes gunning for them, he finds himself in the role of protector to his prime suspect.

*Angela Carlyle*—Jane's roommate ends up dead in the apartment they share, and Jane's the only one who can identify her killer.

*Clint Holbrook*—Who is the steely-eyed man who'll stop at nothing—even murder—to get Jane back under his control?

*Hank Trent*—The Idaho cop has a murder to investigate and a Wyoming cop who's disappeared with his star witness. How many rules will he have to bend to stop the killer before he finds Jane and Joe?

*Harlan Dugan*—The wily old con man claims he can tell Jane who she really is—for a price. But where do his loyalties really lie?

*Melissa Blake*—Joe's stepmother left home when he was just a little boy, breaking his heart. Will she help him now when he needs her the most?

*Riley Patterson*—Joe has always trusted his second-in-command with his life. But can he trust him with Jane's?

# Chapter One

"Tall, dark and cowboy at table four, you lucky dog," Angela Carlyle murmured to Jane as she passed by with the remains of table seven's lunch.

Jane eyed the cowboy in question, taking in his rangy build, short, dark hair and the dun-colored Stetson on the booth next to him. As he glanced her way, she quickly looked back to the older couple perusing their menus. "Our special today is pan-seared trout," she said. "Caught fresh. There's nothing like Idaho trout."

As the couple discussed between themselves the merits of fish for lunch, Jane stole another look at table four. She found the cowboy's gaze fixed on her face, unflinching.

She looked away quickly, unnerved by his scrutiny. She wasn't used to being the object of someone's full attention. Most male customers focused on Angela, with her copper-penny hair, creamy complexion and body even the pale pink waitress uniform couldn't conceal.

Nobody ever stared at Jane, with her face full of freckles, unruly brown hair and slim, not-so-curvy figure. Worse, she was as blank on the inside as she was dull on the outside, with only five months of experiences to call her own and a whole lot of questions she couldn't answer.

"Miss? We're ready."

Jane dragged her gaze away from the cowboy with a soft apology and took their order. She ripped the order from her pad, tucked it in her pocket and crossed to table four.

The cowboy's gray-eyed gaze followed her all the way in. Jane's stomach knotted with vague anxiety. "What can I get you today, sir?" she asked.

"I'll have coffee."

"Sugar or cream?"

His gaze narrowed slightly, as if she'd asked a difficult question. "Just black," he answered.

"We have a trout special, caught fresh this morning—"

"Just coffee," he interrupted, not unkindly.

She nodded. "Coffee it is."

She took his order and the order from the previous table to the kitchen. Angela was there already, cornered by Boyd Jameson, the restaurant manager.

"That's the third order you got wrong," Boyd growled.

"I gave them what they ordered," Angela countered.

"Customer says otherwise and the customer's always—"

"Right," Angela finished for him. "I know. I got them what they wanted immediately and they all gave me big tips, so what's the problem?"

Jane made eye contact with Angela, wondering if she should do something to intervene. Boyd was a piece of work, a real control freak with the waitstaff, and unfortunately, he was untouchable, having worked at the River Lodge longer than most of the staff had been alive.

Angela caught her eye and gave a tiny shake of her head. But it was enough for Boyd to take notice. Whipping his head around, he pinned Jane with his fierce gaze. She looked away, not in any position to cause trouble, and handed off the lunch order to the chef.

She returned to the lunch counter and found the cowboy sitting on a stool in front of her. His dark eyebrows arched slightly when she stumbled to a stop.

"Thought it'd be rude to take up a booth just for coffee." He smiled, but his eyes were watchful.

Unease skittered through her as she poured him a cup of coffee. Placing it in front of him, she plastered on a smile. "Sure I can't get you anything else?"

He eyed her name tag. "What's your last name, Jane?"

She looked down at her hands. "Doe," she answered flatly, wondering if he'd think she was joking.

He was silent a moment. She dared a peek and found him gazing at her through narrowed eyes, one eyebrow quirked. "Nice to meet you, Jane Doe. I'm Joe Garrison." He paused, as if waiting for her reaction.

Was she supposed to react?

Of course she was supposed to react. What kind of guy wouldn't comment on "Jane Doe"?

"Do I know you?" she asked.

His eyes narrowed farther. "Do you?"

She shook her head, her wariness growing. "No. Sorry."

The bell over the front door rang, heralding new customers, a pair of college-age girls dressed for hiking. Grateful for the excuse to walk away, she grabbed a couple of menus and followed as they settled at the booth that Joe Garrison had recently vacated.

She took their drink orders and returned to the counter to fill them. Joe Garrison's gaze followed her as she worked. He didn't even pretend not to stare.

She was about to ask him if he'd like a refill on the coffee when Angela stalked out of the kitchen, her cheeks red with anger. She yanked the strings of her uniform apron and flung the garment onto the counter, stopping next to Jane. "I quit."

Jane looked at her, alarmed. "You what?"

"Quit. Q. U. I. T. Boyd Jameson is a woman-hating jerk, and life is way too short for me to put up with his bull." She started toward the employee break room, but Jane caught her arm.

"Angie, you can't—"

Angela squeezed Jane's arms. "Boyd always had it in for me anyway. There are other jobs. I'll be fine."

*But I won't,* Jane thought, watching her go. Angela was one of the few real friends she'd made in Trinity, Idaho, since she'd turned up wandering through the Sawtooth Mountains a few months earlier, half-frozen and memory-free. She'd gotten used to having Angela around the restaurant as a buffer between herself and Boyd Jameson.

Jane finished the drink orders for table four and turned to Joe Garrison. "Refill?"

"No, thanks. I'm ready for my check."

She didn't know whether she felt relieved or disappointed. As unnerving as Joe's attention might be, it was the first time anyone had ever made her the object of such single-minded focus. Well, that she could remember, anyway. It was flattering, if a bit disconcerting.

She handed him the check. "Hope you enjoy the rest of your day. And come back to see us again."

She carried the drinks to table four. As she took their lunch orders, she caught sight of Joe crossing to the cashier's desk by the door. One of the girls at table four made a low whistling sound. "Look at those jeans," she murmured to her friend.

Jane dragged her gaze away from Joe Garrison's departing backside and returned to the kitchen to hand in the order. When she came back out, Angela stood by the counter, now dressed in jeans and a T-shirt. She gave Jane a quick hug. "I'm heading to the apartment to start making some calls about another job. When do you get off?"

"In an hour. I'll see you there. Maybe we can go for a walk in the park or something, get your mind off things."

"You're on. See you soon."

Jane watched her friend go with a sigh. Behind her, the door from the kitchen swung open with a soft swish. "What're you staring at, Jane? Don't you have customers waiting?" Boyd asked.

She tamped down a smart-alecky comeback that rose in her mind, well aware that she was in no position to be insubordinate. Unlike Angela, she didn't have a lot of other options or the luxury of family in town to help her out if things got tight.

She delivered the food to table six and stopped by one of her other tables to make sure everyone was happy with their orders, then returned to the counter to pick up a pitcher of water to offer refills. As she reached for the ice scoop, she saw that the cowboy had left her a tip. A crisp five-dollar bill—more than three times the cost of the coffee—lay folded neatly on the counter.

Jane had picked it up and started to put it in her pocket when she realized there was something tucked inside. She unfolded the five to discover a business card from the Buena Vista Hotel. He'd written room 225 under the hotel address on the front.

She stared at it, dismayed. Was that the point of his attention? Did he think he could swagger in and pick up the first waitress he set eyes on? Or had he chosen her because she looked particularly easy?

She'd started to crumple the card when she realized there was something written on the back. She flattened it out, staring at the words etched in bold, black strokes.

I know who you are.

The card fell from her suddenly nerveless hands.

THE APARTMENT was small and dingy, smelling of cheap soap and cheaper air freshener. There was only one bedroom and a worn sleeper sofa in the tiny living room. The living room was neat, so Clint guessed she was the one sleeping on the sofa.

He'd taught her all about being neat.

He was tempted to pull the bed out, to see if the sheets tucked inside smelled like her. He refrained, moving instead to the nearest window, carefully parting the curtains and gazing out through the age-warped panes.

The apartment was on the second floor, overlooking a small park across the narrow street. Not much to it, really, a stretch of faded grass and a couple of stubby trees providing shade from the midday sun. It was April in Idaho, still cold enough that most people avoided the shade trees and took full advantage of the sun's mild warmth.

The rattle of the doorknob made him jump. She was early. He'd seen her work schedule when he stopped at the River Lodge Diner for breakfast that morning. She was supposed to be working until one, her roommate until three.

Why was she home early?

Clint skirted the sofa and pressed himself flat against the wall near the door. He didn't want to give her a chance to run.

The door swung open, blocking his view for a moment. It closed and he saw that the unexpected arrival was the roommate, Angela. She'd been his waitress at the diner that morning. No longer in uniform, she wore a figure-hugging T-shirt and low-cut jeans and carried a paper bag full of groceries tucked under one arm.

She turned to engage the dead bolt and stopped short when she caught sight of him. The groceries slipped from her grasp, hit the floor and split open, spilling apples, a head of celery and a box of cereal onto the hardwood floor. She stared at him, recognition dawning in her blue eyes. Then she made a dive for the door.

He stopped her, clamping his hand over her mouth. "We can make this easy or we can make it hard."

She rammed her elbow into his gut and scrambled away. Wincing, he caught her at the kitchen entrance.

"Hard it is," he said, dragging her into the kitchen.

JANE GLANCED over her shoulder for any sign of Boyd Jameson. There was a lull in the lunch crowd, giving Jane a minute to use the pay phone by the kitchen entrance to make her call, but she didn't want Boyd to overhear. Lucky for her, he didn't seem to be around.

"Buena Vista Hotel," a woman's voice answered.

"I'd like to leave a message for Joe Garrison. I believe he's in room 225." Jane kept her voice down.

"Would you like me to check if he's in his room?"

"No," she said quickly. "I just want to leave him a

message. From Jane. He'll know who I am. Tell him I'll meet him at Alliance Park on Briley Street at one-fifteen."

"Alliance Park, one-fifteen."

Jane hung up and grabbed a couple of menus as a pair of hikers entered the restaurant and headed for table six. She took their drink orders, trying to steer her mind away from what she'd just done.

When her shift ended at one, she changed out of her uniform in the employee locker room and donned her sweater and jeans. Not the most appropriate attire for a mysterious assignation, but she wasn't actually going to the park to meet Joe Garrison.

Not yet, anyway.

First, she was going to the Buena Vista Hotel.

THE SECRET to flying under the radar, Jane knew, was to act as if you knew what you were doing at all times. Keep your eyes forward, head up, stride purposeful—not too slow or too fast. Exactly how she knew this, given the vast blank that was her past, she couldn't say, and she had a feeling she wouldn't like the answer if she knew.

She'd spent the last hour at work with half her mind occupied with what to do about Joe Garrison's cryptic note. Meeting him was out of the question. She wasn't about to walk into a trap. She needed to know more about who he was and what he was up to. And that meant getting him out of his hotel room—and herself into it.

She crossed to the pay phone on the lobby wall, put a couple of coins in the slot and dialed the number on the card Joe had given her.

Somewhere behind her, a phone at the front desk rang. A woman answered. "Buena Vista Hotel."

Jane resisted the urge to look behind her at the desk clerk. "This is room number 229. I need housekeeping to bring me extra towels as soon as possible."

"Certainly, ma'am. Right away."

Jane waited a few seconds after the desk clerk rang off before hanging up the pay phone, in case anyone was looking. She crossed to the elevator and hit the button for the second floor.

On the second floor, she stepped out of the elevator and glanced down the hallway. Halfway down, a plump woman with straw-blond hair knocked at a door. "Housekeeping."

Jane started walking down the hall toward her, careful not to look too interested in what the woman was doing. After a few seconds, when there was no answer, the maid pulled out a key, unlocked the door and disappeared inside.

Jane moved quickly then to find room 225. She took a breath and knocked on the door, listening carefully for any sound from within. When she heard nothing, she knocked a little more loudly. "Joe, baby?"

The maid exited room 229 and glanced at Jane.

"Locked myself out." Jane plastered a sheepish smile on her face. "And my husband doesn't seem to be here. I swear, I'm going to have to fit him with one of those tracking devices—"

The maid smiled, lowering her voice. "I have a man like that at home. Want me to let you in?"

"Would you?" Jane didn't hide her excitement, knowing it would help her sell the cover story. "Joe is always teasing me about being a ditz—I'd hate for him to find out I locked myself out of the room! I'd never live it down."

The maid unlocked the door for her. "There you go."

"Thank you so much!" Jane dug in her purse and found a couple of dollars. "Here—for your time."

After the maid left, Jane closed the door behind her and leaned against it, her heart pounding. What the hell had she just done, and how had she known how to do it?

She couldn't give in to her nerves for long. There was no telling how long Joe Garrison would wait for her at the park. She had just a few minutes to look around this place and see if she could figure out exactly who the tall, dark cowboy really was.

The room was unnaturally neat, the suitcase in the bottom of the closet empty. He'd packed his clothes away in the narrow dresser at the foot of the bed, four shirts and four pairs of jeans neatly folded in one drawer, white cotton boxer shorts and white socks carefully lined up in the adjacent drawer.

Pretty buttoned-up for a cowboy.

She spotted a laptop computer on the desk and briefly considered booting it up and taking a look inside, although she had to pause to figure out what, if anything, she knew about computers. But the one thing she did know about them, for sure, was that most people password-protected their systems, and she didn't have time to play hacker, even if she knew how to do it. Which, for all she knew, she did. She seemed to possess some disturbing skills, if her con job with the hotel maid was anything to go by.

She opened the desk drawer. A manila folder lay inside, thick with papers. Taking a deep breath, she pulled out the folder, careful to keep the contents from spilling, and laid it on the laptop.

She pulled up a chair and started scanning the papers. Many were faxes from police departments—Colorado,

Wyoming, Idaho, Kansas—with responses to a request for information about someone named Sandra Dorsey. Caucasian female, midtwenties, five-seven, green eyes, brown hair.

Jane looked up at the mirror over the dresser by the desk. Frightened green eyes stared back at her.

She scanned the faxes for more information. After a few seconds, the rest of the truth became clear. All of the faxes were addressed to Chief Garrison of the Canyon Creek, Wyoming, Police Department.

Chief Joe Garrison.

The cowboy was a cop.

JOE CHECKED his watch. One-fifteen, just as the message had specified. He hadn't figured she'd choose a rendezvous point so close to where she lived, but Trinity, Idaho, wasn't Boise. Everything was close to everything else in a place with only five hundred residents.

Besides, the woman he'd been chasing for months was savvy enough to stick to familiar territory, where she knew all the shortcuts and secret hiding places. She was nothing if not resourceful, or she'd never have evaded him this long.

The Trinity Police Department had cooperated once Joe flashed his badge and briefed them on the case he was working. He'd left out a few details, such as his relationship to the deceased—and to the suspect, short-lived as it had been. But what he'd provided had been enough to ensure that the Trinity police gave him the information he needed to find Sandra's apartment.

Not Sandra, he reminded himself, his mouth tightening into a scowl. Sandra Dorsey was a mirage. Might as well stop thinking of her as a real person.

She was no more real than Jane Doe.

Jane lived in a one-bedroom unit above a hardware store on one of four cross streets intersecting Main. Alliance Park sat directly across the street.

She liked places like that, Joe remembered. She liked bare grass beneath her toes. Fresh air, warm sunshine—

He ruthlessly cut off the images racing through his mind and focused on the job he'd come here to do. He wasn't here to relive a past that he now knew had never been anything more than another of her lies.

He stood inside the hardware store, faking interest in the boxes of nails on the shelf in front of him. Just behind the shelves, the wide picture window gave him an unencumbered view of the park, while the mirror effect of the bright sunshine outside and the relatively darkened interior of the story would hide him from view.

He didn't trust "Jane" to play fairly, especially if she was faking her amnesia. He wasn't about to walk into one of her traps.

He moved slowly up and down the aisle, pretending to read the box descriptions, while the minutes ticked further from their agreed-upon meeting time. By one-thirty, he was beginning to draw the attention of the store employees, but still Jane Doe hadn't shown.

Where the hell was she?

JANE APPROACHED her apartment building from the rear, trying to keep her pace unhurried despite the panic rising like bile in her throat. Angela had shown her how to get inside using the fire escape one day a few weeks ago, when she'd accidentally locked herself out of the apartment. The fire escape landing on the second floor was right outside Angela's bedroom window, which she almost never locked. Not in a place like Trinity.

Jane had thought her roommate was crazy to take such a chance, though she couldn't articulate why. Maybe in her former life, she'd lived in some high-crime district.

Right now, she was glad for a way to get into the apartment without going through the front entrance. The last thing she wanted was to run into Joe Garrison, and there was no way she'd be able to sneak past him. The whole park had a wide-open view of the hardware store.

She took the back steps two at a time and hit the fire-escape ladder running, wincing at the clang of metal against metal as the ladder took her weight. She scrambled up quickly to the landing and pushed open the window, once again grimacing as the aged wood screeched in protest. Slipping as she crawled through the window, she landed gracelessly at the foot of the bed. She looked up, expecting the noise to have brought Angela running.

But her friend didn't appear in the open doorway.

She headed to the living room, stopping short as she caught sight of the spilled bag of groceries lying on the floor in front of the door. "Angie?"

Only silence answered.

She remained still, listening. An odd smell caught her attention. Metallic.

She forced herself to move, edging toward the tiny alcove kitchen. As she stepped into the darkened room, the metallic smell hit her anew. Fear gripped her, cold and darkly familiar, but her mind rebelled against whatever vestige of memory was trying to fight its way to the front of her mind. She turned to run away but her foot slipped from under her and she went down, hitting hard on her side.

She felt something wet beneath her hands. Shaking her hair from her eyes, she saw her roommate's still, bloody body lying tucked up next to the breakfast bar.

She opened her mouth to scream but couldn't find the air for it. A sharp pain lanced through her side.

Then, over the roar of blood pounding in her head, a soft creak behind her made her go still with terror.

"Welcome home, baby."

# Chapter Two

Black flecks danced in front of her eyes as she tried to take a breath. The flecks grew and joined others in a frightening rush, and Jane struggled to sit up, fighting off the darkness.

She drew a deep breath and her vision cleared.

She wished it hadn't.

There was blood everywhere. It covered the faded tile of the kitchenette like spilled milk, pooling in the uneven places and crisscrossing the grout. In contrast, Angela's face was a waxy white, her eyes half-closed, unseeing.

A low noise rumbled from Jane's chest into her throat.

"I didn't want to do it. She wasn't supposed to be here." The voice behind her was low. Male. Smooth and modulated, with a neutral accent she couldn't place.

Jane tried to make herself turn and look at the speaker, but she couldn't move.

"It's time to go, sweetheart." The voice was right behind her. Something soft and smothering whipped down over her head, and her vision went dark again. Strong arms wrapped around her, dragging her to her feet.

The urge to survive overcame the lethargy of grief and

she kicked back hard against her captor's solid form, but he held on tight. She kicked again, making solid contact with his shin. With satisfaction, she heard his grunt of pain and redoubled her efforts.

She managed to free herself and ripped at the cloth covering her face. A pillowcase, she realized, tossing it aside as she raced for the door.

He caught her as she grabbed for the door handle. "No, baby. Shh. Shh." His arms tightened around her, pulling her back against his body. She felt his pulse racing against her shoulder blades. He was breathing hard from the exertion, and she forced down the panic flooding her system. Panic would only weaken her. She had to stay alert. Stay focused. Find his weakness.

She made herself relax in his arms, listening to his breathing, alert to the softening of his grip as she stopped resisting.

His hand smoothed her hair back from where it had fallen in her face. "That's better, baby. See? It's time to go home, sweetheart. You know that. You have something I need."

His voice sounded familiar and foreign at the same time. Confidence tinged every word he spoke. He was a man used to getting his way, unaccustomed to opposition.

She made herself turn slowly in his arms to face him. Hard blue eyes stared down at her from a handsome, even-featured face. A sandy brown mustache and beard covered the lower half of his face. From a distance, it might look real, but as close as she was, she could see that it was a disguise. What she could see of his hair beneath a navy-blue Boise State baseball cap looked to be sandy as well, lighter than the beard.

He wore a black long-sleeved T-shirt and black jeans.

Close up, she could see darker spots that were almost certainly Angela's blood. Her stomach convulsed, and she swallowed hard to keep the bile from rising in her throat.

She forced herself to meet his eyes again. "Where are we going?" she asked.

"Home," he said.

Fear flooded her veins at the simple word. Wherever this man planned to take her, it wasn't a place she'd consider home.

She had to get away from him. Now.

"Home?" she whispered, meeting his eyes. She held his gaze, trying to read his mood, his intentions. He didn't seem to want to kill her here and now, though he clearly had no scruples about murder.

She fought against a rising tide of grief, forcing the sight of Angela's bloody body from her mind. Not now. She couldn't think about it now.

"I kept everything just like you left it," he said, an indulgent tone to his voice. "I watered your jade plant, baby. Just like you used to do it. It's looking good. You'll be pleased when you see it."

The softening of his voice sent a shudder down her spine. He obviously knew her intimately. Was he her husband? Lover? What kind of person had she been, to be intimate with a man who could kill in cold blood?

"I should pack some things," she murmured, trying to keep her voice from shaking.

His eyes narrowed. "I packed for you." He waved his hand to his right. She followed the movement and saw a small bag packed and sitting beside the sofa. She hadn't seen it earlier when she entered from the bedroom. The sofa must have blocked it from view.

"What's my name?" she asked softly.

His eyes narrowed farther. "Don't try to pull that amnesia crap with me, baby. I know your games too well." He turned away from her for a moment, reaching for the bag. It gave her the opening she needed.

As he bent to grab the handle, she pushed him hard, catching him off balance. He lurched forward, hit the coffee table and bounced off the sofa to land on the floor between the two pieces of furniture.

Jane whirled and raced to the door, slamming it behind her as she sprinted down the narrow hallway toward the exit stairs leading down to the hardware store on the first floor. She heard the apartment door open behind her but didn't look back as she jerked open the door to the stairs.

She took the steps at breakneck speed, listening for the sound of pursuit behind her. By the time she reached the first floor, she realized she hadn't heard anyone behind her at all.

But she didn't dare pause to investigate. She burst through the exit door and into the hardware store, her breath coming in short, keening gasps.

Harold, the clerk at the tool desk, looked at her as she ran up to him. His brown eyes widened. "My God, Jane, are you hurt?"

She looked down at her T-shirt and realized it was wet with Angela's blood. The sight made her head swim, and she grabbed at the tool desk, trying to keep her balance. Her hand slipped, painting a crimson streak across the shiny wood as she slid to the floor.

Her world narrowed to a tiny pinpoint of light in a churning sea of darkness. Vaguely, she was aware of Harold's voice as he barked information into the phone.

He must have called 911, she thought, struggling not to drown in the darkness.

Somewhere in the void, a low, familiar voice murmured her name. "Jane."

She stirred, looking toward the voice. The darkness began to recede, and she found herself gazing into the wintry gray eyes of Joe Garrison.

Chief Garrison, she amended mentally, tears burning the backs of her eyes as she met his hard scrutiny.

Unbidden, the words came from somewhere deep inside her, a place she had long feared existed. A place where wariness and suspicion were old, trusted friends.

"I didn't do it," she said.

JOE SLIPPED a pair of plastic covers over the soles of his snakeskin boots and entered the crime scene, crossing to the kitchen alcove where the investigator from the coroner's office was doing the preliminary examination of the body.

Joe introduced himself to the crime scene investigator, Sanderson. "What've we got?"

"Deep incision from the carotid to the jugular. She'd have been dead pretty damn quick." Sanderson glanced up at the rangy lawman standing beside Joe. "Never thought I'd see this in Trinity, Hank."

Chief Hank Trent shook his head. "Neither did I."

Sanderson reached across the body and picked up something lying half-hidden by the body. It was a large filet knife, sticky with blood.

Joe looked up at the kitchen counter and spotted a knife block. There was an empty slot.

"Weapon of opportunity," Chief Trent murmured.

"Guys, I don't want to make your case more compli-cated, but I'm not sure Jane Doe could've done this," Sanderson said quietly. "We'll know more after the autopsy, but this cut looks like it was done in one stroke. Not sure a slip of a woman like the roommate could've made that happen. It probably would've taken a man."

Trent exchanged a look with Joe. "I don't think Ms. Doe needs to know that just yet."

Joe nodded in agreement. "I want to question her."

Trent narrowed his eyes. "This happened in my county, Chief. I get the first crack at her."

"Let me in on it, then."

Trent looked inclined to argue, but after a moment he gave a nod. "I take the lead. Let's not muck this up with interagency squabbling."

"You take the lead," Joe agreed.

"CAN I change out of these clothes?" Jane asked, her posture stiff, as if the feel of the bloody clothes against her skin was painful.

"Soon," Hank Trent promised.

Joe leaned against the wall of the interrogation room, keeping his distance as Hank Trent had requested. He'd listened for the last half hour as the police chief took "Jane Doe" back through the events of that afternoon. It was hard to stay silent with so many questions still unasked, but he wouldn't appreciate an outsider interfering with one of his own investigations, either.

Besides, sooner or later, he'd have his turn with her. And she'd think dealing with Hank Trent was a walk in the park in comparison.

"There was a man in your apartment when you arrived," Trent said for the third time since the interrogation started.

"I told you that already." Her voice rose in frustration. "I've told you what he looked like. I've described his voice. I told you that he had packed a bag for me and expected me to go with him. I told you everything I remember. Can I please just get out of these bloody clothes? Please!" She smacked her hand on the table between them.

"Why'd you bypass the front entrance?" Joe interjected, unable to remain silent any longer.

Both Jane and the police chief turned to look at him.

"You didn't enter the front," Joe said. "I know. I was in the hardware store, watching for you."

Jane's eyes narrowed. She looked back at the chief. "I couldn't find my key," she answered smoothly.

She was a good liar, Joe thought. Believable. But then, he knew that already.

He pulled up a chair and sat by Chief Trent, who shot him a glare. Joe ignored it. He didn't have the time or inclination to play nice with the locals on this case. "Your key was in your purse. Want to try again?"

"I didn't see it in my purse. Why does that matter?" She didn't look so fragile anymore, vibrant color rising in her cheeks and her voice growing hard and tight. She looked more like the woman he remembered from almost a year ago. Images flitted through his mind, daring him to remember her as he'd known her then.

He gritted his teeth and held her angry gaze, replacing the unwanted memories with the stark mental picture of Tommy's lifeless body.

Jane Doe looked at Chief Trent. "Who is this man?"

She didn't say it like someone who wanted an answer, Joe realized. She knew who he was already.

So she *did* remember.

Anger burned in his gut, mingling with the black coffee he'd drunk at the River Lodge Diner. He was beginning to regret skipping breakfast and lunch.

"Chief Garrison is here in Trinity because of you, Ms. Doe. Says you're his prime suspect in a murder in Canyon Creek. Ever been to Canyon Creek?"

When she turned her eyes to meet Joe's gaze, a zing of energy caught him by surprise. Even pale and wary, as she was now, she still possessed the vibrancy he'd noticed the first time he set eyes on her a year ago.

He hated himself for still feeling it.

"Where's Canyon Creek?" she asked.

"Wyoming," Joe answered.

"I hear Wyoming's pretty."

Hank Trent shot a glare at Joe. "I hate to interrupt the travelogue—"

"You spent almost a year in Canyon Creek, Wyoming," Joe continued, ignoring Trent. "You worked for a rancher there. Thomas Blake."

He watched closely for her reaction. Her gaze didn't drop, but he could see her mind working behind those soft green eyes. Was she remembering Tommy's laughter-lined face? The way he could make people feel like family the second he met them?

Was she remembering his body, slumped and still on the stable floor, drenched in the river of crimson flowing from the three bullet holes in his chest?

"We're getting off track here," Hank Trent said firmly. "Chief, unless you'd rather wait outside—"

Joe sat back, knowing he'd crossed a line. This was Trent's territory, and Joe had just trampled all over it. That was no way to make allies of the locals.

And like it or not, he needed allies on this one. He had only the spottiest of evidence against Sandra Dorsey or Jane Doe or whatever the hell her name really was.

But he knew, gut-deep, she was involved with Tommy's murder right down to her pretty little toes.

JANE TUCKED her knees up to her chest, trying to stop crying. Beneath her, the cot was wobbly and hard, but they'd finally let her shower and change into clean clothes. The jail-issued T-shirt and jeans were too large, but at least they weren't covered with Angela's blood.

She closed her eyes tight against the fresh flood of despair. Angie. Why had he killed her? Just because she was in the wrong place at the wrong time?

*My fault,* she thought, rocking back and forth. The mustached man had been there looking for her, not Angie.

*It's time to go home, sweetheart.* That's what he'd said. Home. Was he her husband? Her brother?

No. Not a brother. His gaze had made her feel naked. Exposed. As if he knew everything there was to know about her, inside and out.

What kind of monster had she brought into this sleepy little town?

Footsteps approached her cramped holding cell and came to a stop. Jane forced herself to open her burning eyes, dashing away her tears with her knuckles. Joe Garrison stood just outside her cell, gazing through the bars at her with an expression as intense and knowing as that of the mustached man who'd been waiting in her apartment.

When it became clear he had no intention of speaking first, she asked, "Who are you?"

"You know exactly who I am."

She pushed off the cot and crossed to the bars. He was several inches taller than she was, forcing her to crane her neck to meet his hard gaze. "I know your name. Now I know your job. But I don't know you."

"You're really good, you know?" He raised his arms and gripped the bars over her head, leaning toward her. He seemed to fill all the space in the narrow cell, even though he remained outside. "Even I can't tell if you're lying about not remembering."

Jane gripped the bars in front of her, trying not to let his imposing presence shake her. "Even you?"

His smile was an awful thing. "We go back a ways, Jane. Or is it Sandra?"

Sandra Dorsey, she thought, remembering the name on the papers in Joe's hotel room. "Maybe it's Sandra. I don't know. I don't remember."

"That's convenient." His tight smile widened but grew no warmer. "But unfortunately for you, I don't think it'll be a convincing defense."

"Defense for what?" she asked, not sure she wanted to know the answer.

Joe leaned forward, his face pressed between the bars. "Eight months ago, in Canyon Creek, Wyoming, you killed my brother."

# Chapter Three

Jane's face blanched. She backed away from the bars, groping behind her for the cot, and sat with a graceless thud on the lumpy mattress. "I didn't kill anyone."

"How do you know?" Joe asked, unsurprised by how guileless she sounded. The woman he'd known as Sandra Dorsey had raised sincerity to an art form.

"I couldn't," she insisted, her voice ragged. "I know I couldn't."

The uncertainty in her voice caught him flat-footed. He lowered his voice to a sympathetic murmur. "You don't really know what you would or wouldn't do, do you? Since you don't remember who you are or what life you've lived."

She looked down at her hands, clasping them together to stop their nervous twisting. "I just wouldn't," she muttered stubbornly.

"I've asked the Trinity police to transfer you to my custody for further questioning in Wyoming, but they're not ready to let you out of their jurisdiction yet. Not while there are still questions about your roommate's murder."

She put her hand to her mouth, her face growing even

paler. "Angie," she whispered, tears spilling down her cheeks. "It's my fault, isn't it? He was after me."

Joe gripped the steel bars and watched in silence as she pressed her hands to her face, fresh tears spilling down her cheeks. He hated the rush of sympathy burning a hole in his gut as he watched her obvious distress, hated that even now, he wanted to believe her.

She had a vulnerability about her that drew a man's interest, like a lost little lamb that needed protection. It's what had drawn Tommy to open his home to her and give her a job, no questions asked.

*It's what drew you to her, too,* he mocked himself, tightening his grip on the bars.

"Has Chief Trent found anyone who saw the man in my apartment?" Jane asked, her voice hoarse.

"Not yet."

She looked up at him, biting her lower lip. "You don't think there was a man at all, do you?"

"I didn't say that."

"You didn't have to." She knuckled away her tears, a childlike gesture that made Joe's chest tighten. "You think I killed your brother. What's one more murder?"

He didn't answer, though his gut churned with the need to tell her exactly what he thought of her, what he'd been thinking of her for months as he chased hundreds of dead ends searching for Sandra Dorsey.

"Too bad it messes up your plans to haul me back to Wyoming, right?" A thread of steel hardened her voice as she pushed herself up from the cot and stood to face him. "Were you even going to take me back there? Or were you going to mete out a little frontier justice?"

"I'm not the criminal," he answered tightly, angry at her for even suggesting he'd do such a thing. She knew him better than that.

Or she had. Hell, what if she really wasn't faking the memory loss?

A door opened behind him, dragging his attention away from Jane's hard gaze. Chief Hank Trent entered, a uniformed officer on his heels. He gestured with his head to Joe. "Let's talk."

While Trent pulled Joe to one side, the officer unlocked the holding cell.

"What's going on?" Joe asked.

"We've found a corroborating witness to Ms. Doe's account. I'll explain everything."

"A corroborating witness?" Joe watched Jane exit the holding cell. She met his gaze, her expression tinged with an odd mixture of relief and fear.

"A neighbor saw a man matching the description Ms. Doe gave us. He exited the apartment building by the fire escape," Trent said. "Becker, take Ms. Doe to room three. I need to speak with her further before she's released."

Joe waited until Becker and Jane were out of the room before turning to glare at Hank Trent. "Released?"

"I don't have grounds to hold her."

"Then release her to my custody and I'll take her back to Wyoming on the murder charge."

"There's no murder charge yet. You said that yourself."

"So she just walks around Trinity, scot-free, while two people are dead?"

"She didn't kill Angela Carlyle."

"She killed Thomas Blake."

"You *suspect* she did."

"She had the means and the opportunity. And she ran off the day he died."

"What about motive?"

"I don't have to prove motive."

"And I don't have to turn her over to you." Trent's hard expression softened. "Look, I'm not playing hardball here just to yank your chain. I need her to stick around because she's our best witness in this town's first murder in decades. But I can't keep you from talking to her while you're both here in town."

"You're assuming she'll stick around just because you tell her to."

Trent smiled. "Well, I've arranged a little something for Ms. Doe that just might interest you."

"THE BUENA VISTA HOTEL?" Jane stared at Hank Trent as if he were crazy. She glared at Joe. "This is your idea, isn't it?"

Joe shook his head. "You're a murder witness and the perpetrator is still at large. You need protection, and the Trinity police know the Buena Vista Hotel has the best security in town."

Jane shook her head, thinking how easily she'd talked her way into Joe Garrison's room earlier that day. "That's not saying much."

Trent made an exaggerated huffing sound.

"Chief Trent has arranged for your room to be next to mine," Joe said softly, drawing her gaze. His cool gray eyes held hers, full of challenge.

"I just bet he did," she muttered.

"We don't have officers to spare, with a murderer at large," Chief Trent said, his tone annoyingly reasonable.

"Chief Garrison was kind enough to offer his services as your security guard. You won't get a better offer."

Jane tugged at the neck of her T-shirt. "What's keeping me from packing my bags and getting the hell out of this town? If I'm not under arrest."

"We can hold you for twenty-four hours without charging you with anything, you know." Trent's voice hardened. "I'd prefer that you cooperate voluntarily."

"I've told you all I know."

"Then consider this," Joe interjected, pulling up the chair across the table from her. He turned it around and straddled it, resting his arms across the rounded back and pinning her with his hard gaze. "There's a guy running around out there who didn't think twice about slitting your friend's throat because she got in his way. And from what you tell us, he wants you. Do you really want to be out there on your own right now?"

Jane looked down at the scuffed table, running her finger over a nick as she tamped down a flood of fear at his words. "No."

"Then the Buena Vista it is." Trent slapped his hand on the table, sealing the deal.

Jane bit her lower lip, her insides twisting into a painful knot. She felt trapped, shackled by the iron will of the lawmen and by her own blank memory.

"I'll make the arrangements." Trent rose and headed out of the interrogation room, leaving Jane alone with Joe Garrison. Joe gazed at her over his folded arms, clearly content to let her squirm beneath his scrutiny.

"Do you usually get your way?" She couldn't keep a thread of bitterness out of her voice.

"No," he answered.

"I don't believe that."

"If I always got my way, my brother wouldn't be dead and I wouldn't be here in Trinity babysitting the last person to see him alive."

"Who was I to your brother?" she asked, fearing the answer.

Joe dropped his gaze for the first time, focusing on the nicked wood tabletop. "You worked for him."

"Doing what?"

He looked up sharply at her wary tone. "You kept his house for him. Helped him with the business end of the ranch. Odd jobs—whatever he needed done."

She took a deep breath and asked the question she dreaded most. "Were he and I…"

Joe shook his head. "No. He was a recent widower. Not over his wife's death yet. You were…friends."

She didn't miss the bitterness of his tone. "Or so he thought, huh? Isn't that what you're thinking?"

"You tell me."

"I don't remember."

"I don't believe you."

She slapped her hands on the table in front of her, venting her frustration. Her palms stung and she balled her hands into fists. "Why? What did I do to you to make you believe I'd kill your brother? That I'd lie about not remembering?"

"Because you lied about who you were, for one thing." His voice was quiet. Calm. But she heard anger roiling beneath the placid surface. It made her feel queasy.

"How do you know?" She couldn't help but lean closer to him, eagerness overcoming wariness. "Do you know who I really am?"

He leaned away from her, his knuckles whitening as he

gripped the back of his chair. "No. I just know you're not someone named Sandra Dorsey. The Social Security number you gave Tommy belonged to a deceased woman by the same name."

"Do you think I killed her, too?"

The corner of his mouth quirked. "No. Sandra Dorsey died in a car accident in Trenton, New Jersey, four years ago. I think you paid someone to give you a new identity, and they stole her name and Social Security number to make you into a new person."

Jane looked away from his hard gaze, her chest tight with tension. Why had she gone to such obvious trouble to change her identity? What kind of woman was she?

"The man you saw at your apartment—did he seem familiar to you?" Joe asked.

"No. But he knew me." She forced herself to look at him. "Do you know who he is?"

Joe shook his head. "No. I don't."

"Maybe he's the one who killed your brother."

"Maybe that's what you'd like me to believe."

"And you won't even entertain the possibility that I wasn't the one who killed him."

"You disappeared the day he died. You were gone by the time the neighbor found Tommy's body." He stumbled over the words, his gaze dropping away.

Jane felt the ridiculous urge to reach across the table and put her hand over his, to lend him what little strength and comfort she had.

He took a deep breath and continued, his voice threaded with steel. "Your bags were gone. Your clothes. Every-thing. It was like you'd never been there in the first place."

"That was eight months ago, right?"

Joe nodded.

"So, where was I between then and this past December when I showed up here in Trinity?"

"I don't know yet."

"How'd you find me?"

"I got a fax from the Trinity Police Department, seeking information on a Jane Doe."

The door to the interview room opened, and Chief Trent walked in before Jane could respond. "All set. I'm afraid we have to keep the bag we found packed in your living room. For evidence."

"What do I do for clothes?" she asked.

"My sister Erica runs clothing drives for one of the local churches. She's agreed to raid their stash for a few things your size," Chief Trent answered. "She's left it for us at the hotel."

"Ready to go, then?" Joe asked.

She frowned at the impatience in his voice but gave a swift nod, falling in step in front of him as they followed the police chief out of the room.

BY THE TIME Joe led Jane from the police station, the sun had dipped behind the Sawtooth Mountains, leaving only a faint orange glow in the western sky. Streetlamps along the town's main streets had already come on, battling the chilly gloom of twilight.

Joe motioned toward his truck, parked in a visitor slot in front of the station. Jane managed a weak smile. "Did you drive over from Wyoming or did you rent that truck at the Boise airport?"

"I drove," he answered tersely.

Her forehead creased. "Did I say something wrong?"

"No." He couldn't exactly tell her that she used to tease him about his truck and his Stetson and everything that went with being a Wyoming cowboy. Back then, she'd said it with such affection he found himself laughing with her. Now he wondered if it had all been an act, all the smiles and the jokes and the easy charm. He hated not knowing what was real and what was a lie.

Maybe the smartest way to deal with her was to assume everything that came out of her mouth was some sort of lie.

"Could we stop by the River Lodge Diner?" she asked as she climbed into the passenger seat of the Silverado.

"Why?" he asked as he settled behind the wheel.

"I want to let my friend Doris at the diner know I'm okay." She buckled her seat belt and looked across at him. "She'll know about Angie by now, and she'll probably be worried about me."

There was a hint of wonder in her voice, as if she was surprised to know someone cared about what happened to her. He recognized the look. He'd seen it on her face when he first met her almost two years ago, as she told him about the way Tommy had taken her in, no questions asked, when she showed up on his doorstep needing help.

Tommy should've asked questions.

They all should've.

He started the truck and gave a brief nod. "The River Lodge Diner it is."

"Oh, Janie!" Doris Bradley engulfed her in a bear hug as soon as Jane entered the diner, drawing the curious gazes of the handful of customers who'd opted for the diner's home cooking rather than the lodge restaurant's more cosmopolitan fare. Her eyes were red-rimmed from crying.

"I've been worried sick about you ever since we heard the news about Angie."

"I'm okay, Doris," Jane assured her. "But I'm not going to be able to work for a while. Boyd's going to have to find two new waitresses, I'm afraid."

"You can't work? Why not?" Doris stepped back, holding Jane by the shoulders. She looked her up and down. "You're not hurt, are you?"

"No, I'm fine!" Jane glanced at Joe, who stood a few paces away, watching her with hard gray eyes. She'd asked him not to tell anyone at the diner about her involvement in the case, and he'd agreed, but she didn't know if she could really trust him to keep his word.

He'd lied to her more than once already, however good his reasons might have been.

"Is Boyd here?" she asked Doris. "I guess I should really tell him myself."

"Sorry, hon. Boyd hasn't been here all afternoon. He got a call from his sister a little after one." Doris lowered her voice to a half whisper. "I think maybe she's having another one of her episodes. You know he doesn't like to talk about it."

"I guess I'll just have to drop by tomorrow sometime. I'll need to pick up my last paycheck anyway." She gave Doris another hug and turned to look at Joe again.

"Ready to go?" he asked.

She felt Doris's curious gaze on her, but she didn't stop to explain. She could hardly tell her co-worker that she was basically under house arrest at the Buena Vista Hotel under the watchful eye of Cowboy Joe. Word about her situation would get around soon enough as it was.

"Episodes?" Joe asked as they headed away from the diner toward the Buena Vista.

"What?"

"Your boss's sister has episodes?"

"Oh. She's a paranoid schizophrenic. She does well when she stays on her medication, but she doesn't always stay on it. Boyd's all she has in the world, and as big a jerk as he can be, he works himself to the ground to help her have some sort of normal life. So when she calls—"

"He goes running," Joe finished for her.

She glanced at his profile, outlined by the yellow glow of streetlamps lining Main Street. "Family, I guess."

He cut his eyes her way. "Family," he agreed.

The well-lit facade of the Buena Vista Hotel shimmered against the dark blue backdrop of the Sawtooth Mountains as Joe pulled the truck into the guest parking lot. He unbuckled his seat belt and turned to look at her. "I know I've made it pretty clear that I don't think you're telling me the truth. About your memory or about what happened a year ago or six hours ago."

"No! Really?"

"But I don't believe you were the one who killed Angela Carlyle. The evidence argues against it."

She felt a ripple of relief. "So you believe me about the man?"

"I believe a man killed your roommate. Who or what he is to you is still a question."

"For me, too."

He shot her a sidelong look. "My point is, the man is still at large, and if you're the only witness to his murder of your friend, he might want to shut you up."

She tamped down a shudder. "You think I don't know that?"

"I think you need a reminder. I know firsthand that you have a tendency to run."

She opened her car door and stepped out, turning to look at him through the open door. "I'm not stupid. I know I'm not safe out there on my own. That's why I agreed to this setup."

"Good. Then we're on the same page."

She closed the door a little harder than necessary. "We'll never be on the same page, cowboy," she muttered.

She followed him into the hotel and waited impatiently while he picked up the key to her room from the desk clerk. "You're in room 223. It's an adjoining room to mine."

"Adjoining?"

"You know, there's a connecting door between our rooms?"

"I know what adjoining means." She frowned at him as they entered the elevator. "I just wondered why."

"Easy access," he answered cryptically.

"I'm surprised you didn't request that Chief Trent just put me in your room with you. Maybe supply you with a set of handcuffs to chain me to the bed or something."

"I did. He nixed it. But I have my own set of cuffs if you're interested."

She looked up sharply, surprised at the hint of humor she heard in his deep, gravelly voice. "My God, that was a joke, wasn't it? Cowboy Joe just told a joke."

The half smile quirking his lips faded and his gray eyes darkened. "Don't get used to it."

She sighed as the elevator lurched and settled on the second floor. The door swished open and she started to step out, but Joe swung his arm out, stopping her.

"Let me check it out first." Holding the doors open with one hand, he stuck his head out of the elevator and looked both ways. "Okay, let's go."

She followed him into the deserted hallway, remembering her earlier visit to his hotel room. What would Joe say if he knew she'd been here already, conned her way inside his room and gone through his things? Check that. She had a feeling she already knew what he'd say.

Joe stopped in front of room 223 and swiped the card key in the lock, opening the door. Jane took a step inside ahead of him and stopped dead in her tracks.

Behind her, Joe uttered a low profanity.

Spread across the bed, in the unmistakable shape of a body, lay hundreds of blood-red rose petals.

## Chapter Four

Trinity Police Chief Hank Trent took one look at the rose-strewn hotel bed and uttered a scalding string of epithets.

"We can't stay here," Joe said when he was done.

"I'll find you another hotel."

"We can't stay here in Trinity," Joe said firmly.

"You expect me to just let you waltz out of town with my only eyewitness to a murder?"

Joe glanced at the Jane. She stood a few feet away, her gaze still fixed on the rose-petal effigy posed like a crimson corpse on the pale bedspread. She had said almost nothing since they'd opened the hotel room door, but her distress was evident in her pale face and wide, haunted eyes.

"The only people who knew we were coming here besides Jane and me were you and your department, Chief." Joe turned his gaze to Trent. "She was in your custody the whole time."

"You weren't."

"You want to check my credentials again?"

Trent frowned. "No. Just guarantee me you're not pulling some fast one here to get her back to Wyoming."

"I just want to keep her alive until we can figure out

what the hell is going on here," Joe assured him. "I'll take her somewhere safe and get back in touch with you directly to let you know where we are."

Though his face reflected his reluctance, Trent gave a grudging nod. "Stay in this state, Garrison. I mean it."

Joe nodded. "I'll be in touch as soon as we settle somewhere." He crossed to Jane and touched her elbow.

She gave a little jerk and turned startled green eyes to him. "What's happening now?"

"I'm taking you out of town."

Her eyes darkened with suspicion. "To Wyoming?"

"No. We have to stay in Idaho."

"But not here."

He cupped her elbow in his palm, trying to ignore the way her warmth seeped into his bloodstream and settled in the center of his chest, the way it had always done, right from the start. He led her out into the hallway, away from the handful of police and technicians examining the hotel room for evidence. "You're not safe here."

She looked away. "I'm not safe anywhere."

"Why do you say that?" he asked, tightening his grip on her elbow.

She pulled her arm from his grasp. "Just a feeling."

"Not a memory?"

She met his gaze again. "Not a memory."

"You don't remember anything."

She shook her head.

If she was faking, she was amazingly consistent about it. He'd watched her carefully over the past few hours as she dealt with the aftermath of her friend's murder, and not once had she slipped.

He picked up the small suitcase filled with women's

clothes Hank Trent's sister had brought for Jane, nodding for her to follow him to his room. He closed the door behind them and turned to look at her. She looked even more wary and pale. "Are you okay?"

She gave a brief nod.

He motioned toward the chair next to the bed. "Sit down before you fall down."

She obeyed, tucking her feet up and wrapping her arms around her knees. She looked so much thinner than he remembered. Fragile, almost. A fist of tension formed in the center of his chest and he forced himself not to cross to her side and pull her into his arms.

Once, he'd have done so, without hesitation. But that time seemed like decades ago, not just a short, harrowing eight months. The woman he'd known in Canyon Creek had been an illusion.

He'd thought he could trust her, just like he'd thought he could trust his stepmother. Like he'd thought he could trust Rita. But they'd left him, just like the woman he'd known as Sandra.

Women couldn't be trusted. He couldn't let himself forget it.

"Where are you taking me?" Jane asked, her voice raspy.

"I don't know. I thought we'd head to Boise and decide from there."

"Why are you trying to protect me?" She turned her wide-eyed gaze on him again.

He swallowed a rush of pure, masculine desire and looked away. "It's my job."

"No, it's Chief Trent's job."

"I need answers," he admitted after a brief pause. "I need to know exactly what happened the day Tommy died."

"I thought you already knew."

A knock at the door kept him from having to say more. He found Hank Trent standing outside. "Just thought you'd want to know that the FBI resident agency in Idaho Falls has offered the services of a profiler on this case. I don't have a good reason to say no."

Probably not a bad idea to have a profiler on this, Joe had to admit, though he generally didn't like the feds nosing around on a case he was working. But that would be Trent's headache, not his. Joe turned to Jane. "You ready?"

She picked up the suitcase he'd set by the bed and squared her jaw. "Let's do it."

He shook Trent's hand, promised to be in touch and led Jane down to the hotel parking lot.

CLINT SLOWLY approached the Chevy Silverado parked in the hotel lot, taking in the Wyoming plates. So Joe Garrison was in town.

"Guess you got the memo, too," he murmured wryly. He should have figured. But the cowboy was out of luck this time. He could swagger around in his stupid hat and his Wrangler jeans, but it would make no difference. Clint was no steer to be wrangled into submission nor a horse to be broken. He wouldn't let a two-bit hayseed hick keep him from getting what he came to Idaho to retrieve.

He stuck the device to the Silverado's undercarriage, just behind the passenger door, and straightened, dusting off his hands and tugging at the folds of his dark trench coat. He slipped into the shadows as two people emerged from the hotel and headed for the parking lot.

From his hiding place behind a mud-splattered Dodge Durango, he watched Joe Garrison open the door for Jane and help her into the truck. What a gentleman. His lip curled in a sneer at the thought.

He let them drive away before he emerged from the shadows and crossed slowly to the Lexus he'd rented at the airport in Boise. He took his time, placing a call that would put the next phase of his plan into motion. Then he pulled out his palm-size computer and checked the status of the device he'd placed on Joe Garrison's truck.

The signal was strong and clear.

He smiled.

"WHAT KIND of provisions can we find here?" Jane looked at the gas-station food mart, skeptical. They were about thirty minutes out of Trinity, still on the main highway to Boise.

"Food. Water. I thought we might find a couple of prepaid disposable cell phones to make it hard to trace any calls we have to make. I have a first-aid kit but it wouldn't hurt to stock up on extra supplies—aspirin, antihistamine cream, antibiotic ointment—"

"Are we going to need those?"

"Be prepared."

She couldn't stop a soft giggle. "Should've known you were a Boy Scout."

He looked up sharply. "You remember Boy Scouts?"

She frowned. "I guess I do. I mean, I know what they are. I think."

She didn't like the suspicion in his eyes as he studied her face. He made her feel like a chronic liar, the way he looked for subterfuge in everything she said or did. Was he that way with everyone? She supposed, being a cop, he had to be skeptical by nature, but she didn't like being the focus of so much disbelief.

It made her wonder if she deserved it.

The worst thing about not remembering her past was not knowing what kind of person she really was. People these days were big on the idea that the past didn't matter, only the present and the future. Angela had even expressed envy, seeing in Jane's situation a golden opportunity to wipe the slate clean—whatever her past had been—and start fresh as a brand-new person.

Easy to say when it was someone else's past that was erased. Not so easy when you had to create a life, a personality, out of nothing but a complete blank.

She didn't wait for Joe to open the door for her, meeting him in front of the truck. "I guess we should concentrate on food staples, since we don't know how long we'll be out here on our own, huh?"

"Yeah." For once, there was something besides suspicion in his gray eyes. Was it admiration? She didn't dare hope.

She followed him into the food mart. "Why don't we split up? It'll go faster that way. I'll get the food, you get the other supplies—"

"No. We stick together," he said firmly.

And the suspicion was back, she thought. She sighed as he picked up a shopping basket and headed down the first aisle. She grabbed a basket of her own and fell into step with him.

She picked up a jar of outrageously expensive peanut butter and put it in the basket. "A grocery store would've been a whole lot cheaper."

"And more exposed."

His dead-serious tone unnerved her. "You're trying to scare me now."

"You're not scared already?" He glanced her way.

"Okay, you're trying to scare me more."

He dropped a large loaf of bread into the basket and headed for the drink coolers at the end of the aisle, not answering.

By the time they reached the checkout stand, both of their baskets were full. Joe paid the bill with a credit card and turned to Jane. He handed her his keys. "I'll get the bags. You get the doors." He took the two full sacks of provisions from the cashier and followed her outside.

Jane unlocked the passenger door for him and took one of the bags, sliding it into the narrow space behind the seats. As she took the other bag from him, Joe suddenly lurched toward her with a low grunt. Almost simultaneously, she heard a loud thumping sound and the whole truck shook.

"Joe?"

Joe closed his fingers around her arm, the grip painfully tight. "Get in the truck!" he growled.

She pulled up into the cab. A loud *thunk* shook the truck again, and Joe pushed her to keep going.

"Get behind the wheel!" He pushed her until she crawled over the storage console and settled behind the wheel. Joe hauled himself into the passenger seat and slumped low. "Drive!"

She fumbled the key into the ignition and started the truck. "What's going on?"

Another metallic thud made the truck rock. Joe grabbed her arm and squeezed. "Just drive, damn it!"

She put the truck in gear and pulled onto the highway, realization settling over her in cold waves. "Someone was shooting at us."

Joe remained silent. She shot a look at him, alarmed by the way he lay half-sprawled across the seat. "Are you all right?"

"I'm fine," he gritted in a tone that told her he was anything but.

Her heart dropped. "You got hit."

"I don't think it's bad."

Jane gripped the steering wheel and pressed the pedal to the floor. "God, where's the nearest hospital? Maybe we should stop and call 911—"

"No!" Joe pushed himself up to a straighter sitting position. "No paramedics. It's not that bad."

She flicked on the interior light and he squinted at her, his face pale and sweaty. "Not that bad?"

"Just—the next wide place on the shoulder, pull off. Okay? And turn off that light!"

She turned it off, plunging the interior of the truck cab into darkness again. She could hear Joe's soft pants of pain and considered defying his wishes. But then she spotted a widening of the shoulder straight ahead and slowed to pull to the side of the highway. She put the truck in Park and turned to Joe. "What now?"

"I need you to get out of the truck and start feeling around the undercarriage."

"What?"

"Just do it!" He took a couple of swift, shallow breaths and added, "Please?"

Jane cut the engine and got out of the truck. She left the door open so she could hear Joe. "What am I looking for?"

"Anything stuck to the truck's underside that doesn't feel like it belongs," he answered, his voice thready.

*That's helpful,* she thought. She ran her hands along the

undercarriage from the back of the truck to the front bumper. "Nothing so far."

"Keep going."

She felt her way around the front of the truck and started down the passenger side. Just behind the passenger door, her fingers ran into something hard and cold. "I think I found something."

Joe lowered the window. "Can you pull it away from the truck?"

She jerked her hand away, a sudden, horrifying thought darting through her mind. "Is it a bomb?"

"I doubt it. Why shoot at us if we were rigged to blow?" Joe leaned his head against the window frame. "Just see if you can pull it off."

She reached under the truck, grabbed the edges of the square object and gave a tug. It popped free and she stood up straight, holding it out for Joe to see.

He took it from her and studied it in the pale glow of the truck's dome light. Muttering a soft curse, he handed it back to her. "Throw it as far away as you can."

"What is it?"

"Just throw it away and get back in the truck. We need to get a move on."

Biting back her irritation, she hurled the small metal box into the scrubby underbrush lining the highway, then slid behind the steering wheel. "Done. Now, are you going to tell me what the hell that was?"

"It was a GPS tracker."

It took a second to place what he was talking about. "Someone was tracking us? Who?"

"That's the question, isn't it?" He reached for the seat belt, grimacing as he tried to slip the metal tab into the buckle.

Jane reached across and buckled the belt for him. She took a moment to adjust her own seat forward so she could better reach the pedals. Taking a couple of slow, deep breaths to fight the flood of adrenaline coursing through her bloodstream, she pulled onto the highway. "So, what do we do now?"

"We don't keep going to Boise," Joe said. "We need to find a place that nobody would think to connect to either of us."

"Somewhere secluded?" she asked, her mind racing to think of an answer.

"Yeah."

The problem was, she was almost as much a stranger to the area as he was. She'd spent most of the past five months in the little apartment she'd shared with Angie. Most of her trips out of town had been doctor's appointments in Ketchum or the occasional day trip to Boise. The only time she'd spent more than a few hours out of town had been the previous Christmas, when Angie had invited her to spend the holiday with her family up at their cabin in the Sawtooth Mountains—the cabin!

"I know a place," she said aloud.

THOUGH JANE had closed the door to the tiny bathroom, Joe couldn't miss the retching sounds. He had to hand it to her, however; she'd made it through the nasty job of cleaning up and binding his gunshot wound before her stomach finally rebelled.

He pressed his hand to his aching side, where Jane had carefully picked singed pieces of his shirt from his ragged bullet wound, then bandaged him with what he suspected was a sanitary napkin, although he hadn't wanted to ask. At this point he hurt too much to care.

He heard the bathroom door open and Jane's soft footfalls moving up behind him. She smelled like mint toothpaste and soap. He pushed himself up to a wobbly sitting position to watch her approach.

She sat next to him. "You still hanging in there?"

Her hip pressed against his, warm and soft. It chased away some of the chill that had wrapped itself around him like a shroud. "Yep."

She brushed his hair back from his forehead, her touch soothing. Now that she was closer, he could smell the soft, clean scent that belonged to her alone. He breathed as deeply as he dared, filling his lungs with her. Filling his muddled mind with memories.

"Do you remember—" he started, then caught himself. "'Course you don't remember. You don't remember anything." His brain was beginning to feel fuzzy.

"Shh," she soothed him, laying the back of her hand on his forehead. "You need to try to sleep."

He caught her hand and squeezed. "The room's spinning."

Her lips curved slightly, prompting him to try to remember what she looked like with a full smile. "Joe, let's lie down now—"

He let go of her hand and curled his palm around the back of her neck, ignoring the jolt of pain in his side. "Let's do," he said, pulling her to him.

She tumbled against his chest, her hands flattening against his chest. "Joe—"

He shushed her with his mouth.

## Chapter Five

He tasted of heat and a hint of bourbon from the couple of sips she'd given him from the Carlyle family stock before she cleaned his wound. Her head swam and her whole body seemed to go tingly and numb as his tongue danced against hers in a deep, shattering kiss.

He slid his hands lazily down her back, his fingertips tracing the contours of her spine in slow, deliberate circles. Heat poured into her center, sheer sensation driving her as she straddled his hips and pressed hard against him, seeking more.

But as her whole body burst into flaming need, his hands slackened against her back and slid away. His mouth went soft beneath hers.

She pulled away and pushed her tangled hair out of her eyes, gazing down at him. His eyes were closed, his mouth still slightly open and glistening with the moisture of their kisses. His breathing was slow and even, and when she touched his bare chest, she felt his pulse strong and rhythmic beneath her fingertips. He was just asleep, she reassured herself.

A low, unsteady chuckle escaped her as she pushed

herself off him and retreated to a chair a few feet away from the bed. Her body still thrummed with arousal, but she pushed away the sensation ruthlessly, closing her eyes against the sight of Joe's bare, toned torso and tight jeans that revealed arousal, even now. He shifted slightly in the bed, a low sound grumbling up from his chest.

*Bet you're having a hell of a dream right now, Cowboy Joe,* she thought, chuckling again.

A word spilled from his lips, whispery and taut with need. "Sandra."

Jane's chuckle died in her throat.

*Sandra.* That was the name she'd used in Wyoming, wasn't it?

She pushed herself from the chair and crossed back to the bed, easing herself down on the edge next to him. "Joe?"

"Sandra, don't leave me." The words were slurred but discernible. He shook his head from side to side, his face crumpling with pain. "Don't—"

"Shh." She touched his forehead, soothing away the creases. "I'm right here."

The lines in his brow relaxed, and he fell still and silent. She sat by his side a few minutes longer, trying to hold back the sudden panic rising in her throat like a tidal wave.

His voice had sounded—distant, somehow. As if whatever he was dreaming about came from the past, not the present. A past where he had known her as Sandra Dorsey, not Jane Doe.

A past that had suddenly become even more complicated than she'd imagined.

Exactly who—and what—was she to Joe Garrison?

MORNING DAWNED cold and clear, the first gray whisper of daylight stealing over the bedroom where Jane sat, wide-awake, watching Joe sleep. She rubbed her gritty eyes and checked her watch in the low light, barely making out the numbers. Just after five.

Joe had slept most of the night, awakening briefly around three to go to the bathroom. He'd waved off her offer of help on the way in, but when he emerged, white-faced and staggering, he didn't protest when she wrapped her arm around him and helped him back to bed.

That moment was the only reason she was still here, sitting in the darkened bedroom listening to his slow, even respiration. She'd planned to be gone by morning. She'd gone as far as sneaking the truck keys from his jacket to the pocket of her jeans, where even now they dug into her hip through the sturdy denim.

Angie was dead. Joe was injured. And as far as she could see into her uncertain future, she didn't think things would get any better for the people around her.

Maybe, if she could still see Joe Garrison as a Wyoming cop who wanted her behind bars, she could forget those fears and trust Joe to help her.

But the kiss had changed everything.

Wrapping herself in the wool blanket she'd had across her lap, she crossed to check the woodstove in the corner. The fire she'd lit last night had waned, the two small logs she'd found inside now mostly burned away to ashes. The cabin had electricity but not heat. Angie's family usually brought portable space heaters to supplement the fireplace in the great room and the single woodstove located here in the back bedroom.

She returned to the bed and looked down at Joe. He lay on his uninjured side, his face buried in the pillow. He looked like a little boy, his features softened by sleep and his dark hair flopping forward onto his forehead. Such a contrast to the hard, grim man who'd confronted her at the Trinity jail.

She crouched by the bed in front of him, gripping the sheets to keep from reaching out to touch him. "Who are you to me?" she whispered.

He stirred slightly, and she rocked back on her heels, holding her breath until he settled back to sleep. Carefully, she pushed to her feet and picked up her boots, tucking them under her arm as she padded barefoot into the great room. She pulled them on and stood, gazing at the front door of the cabin.

She reached into her pocket and closed her fingers around the keys to Joe's truck.

JOE WOKE with a start, then immediately regretted it as pain shot through his body.

It took a moment for memory to seep through his pain-addled brain. When it did, he forced himself to a full sitting position and looked around the darkened bedroom.

Morning sunlight crept through the curtains, slanting a weak shaft of light across the hardwood floor. Joe ran his hand over his jawline, feeling the full day's growth of beard, then checked his watch. Ten after seven. His stomach rumbled, but not with hunger.

"Jane?" His voice sounded gravelly and weak. He called her name again, louder this time, but there was no response.

Alarm battled with anger as he swung his legs over the side of the bed and sat there a moment, clutching the bedsheets in his white-knuckled fists as he waited out the rush of pain and nausea. He listened to the quiet cabin, trying to make out any unexpected sounds. Cold air swirled around him, raising chill bumps on his bare skin. He needed to go to the bathroom but pushed that concern aside and struggled to his feet.

The room swam sickeningly for a moment, but he pressed his hand against the wall for balance and grabbed the tattered remains of his cotton button-down shirt. He slipped it on, favoring his injured side, and looked down at his boots standing at the side of the bed.

No way could he put those boots on alone, and Jane knew it. Probably thought it would give her a head start.

He picked up his jacket from a chair near the bed. A pair of bullet holes marred the left side of the tan suede. He fingered one of the holes briefly, then pulled on the jacket, reaching into the pocket for his truck keys.

They were gone.

He released a soft torrent of curses and headed out the bedroom door, staggering a bit as he moved down the short hallway to the great room. He went straight for the front door and parted the curtains over the inset window.

The truck stood where they'd left it the night before.

Releasing a pent-up breath, he leaned against the door, letting it hold him upright while he gritted his teeth against the pain in his side.

So she hadn't taken the truck.

But where was she?

FROST COVERED the ground outside the cabin, tinted shell-pink by the glow that kissed the eastern sky. The sun had not yet made an appearance over the Sawtooth Mountains, but the light on the horizon was enough to illuminate the small stockpile of firewood stacked on the side porch.

Jane pulled on a pair of work gloves she'd found in the kitchen and started to reach for the top piece of wood when she heard a snapping sound in the tangle of pines and aspens a few yards away.

She peered into the gloom, the hair on the back of her neck rising. She eased her hand into the pocket of her jacket, where she'd tucked Joe's service weapon before leaving the cabin, and pulled it free. Pressing her back against the rough clapboard of the cabin's outer wall, she held her breath and tried to be completely still and invisible, watching the trees for any sign of movement.

She heard a soft rustle, then another twig snapping. Two shadowy figures slunk through the scrubby underbrush, flitting in and out of sight. Jane released her breath and the shadows froze, two pairs of bright gold eyes turned her way.

Wolves. They stared back at her briefly before slipping away, wraithlike, in the gloom.

Jane crossed to the edge of the porch, trying to catch another glimpse of them as they retreated, but they had already disappeared from view. She started to turn back to the woodpile when she heard a creaking noise behind her. Her heart rate doubling in a split second, she whipped the gun up, whirled and aimed.

Joe stood in the doorway, his hands lifting slowly. His gaze locked with hers, hard and wary. "Drop the weapon, Jane."

She swallowed hard and lowered the gun to her side. "You scared the hell out of me."

"Likewise," he drawled, taking a step toward her and holding out his hand. "I'd like it back now."

She didn't like the dark suspicion in his eyes. "Did you think I would shoot you?"

"People don't usually aim a weapon if they're not prepared to pull the trigger."

She pressed her lips together, annoyed by his dry half answer. She handed him the gun and turned to pick up a couple of pieces of wood for the stove. But he caught her arm and pulled her around to face him.

"So, you're only out here for the wood?" He held her by her upper arms, his grip painless but firm.

She lifted her chin. "I'm out here for the wood."

He stepped forward, forcing her back up against the wall of the cabin. Heat radiated off his body, warming her through the denim of her jacket and jeans. He smelled of whiskey and woodsmoke, the scent rich, dark and masculine. She pressed her hands flat against the rough wall, overwhelmed by the urge to touch him.

He snaked his left hand out and curled his palm around her waist. He slid his fingers slowly, deliberately over the curve of her hip, stopping at the pocket of her jeans and tracing the contours of the bulge inside. "So why did you need the keys to my truck, then?"

She dropped her gaze, knowing she had no good answer.

He let go of her and stepped back, throwing up a hand to catch the wall as he struggled with his balance. His voice shook when he spoke. "I guess the more pertinent question is, why didn't you run when you had the chance? I was dead to the world. Would have been so easy."

She pushed her hair away from her face, surprised to find her hand trembling. She could still feel the phantom heat of his hand on her hip. Pulling the keys from her pocket, she licked her dry lips and handed them to Joe. "Where would I go? I don't know anyone outside of Trinity. I don't know any *place* outside of Trinity."

"I have a feeling you could adapt."

"I didn't want to leave you," she blurted, forcing her gaze up to meet his.

For a second, she thought she saw a flicker of pleasure dart across his expression, but it was gone before she could be sure what she saw. He put his keys in the pocket of his jeans and started to pick up a piece of wood.

She put her hand over his, stopping him. He looked up at her, his eyes narrowing.

"I'll get it. You're still a little weak." She tucked a couple of pieces of wood under her arm and cupped his elbow to help him inside the cabin.

He shrugged her off. "I'm fine."

She let him go ahead of her, watching with concern as he made his way on wobbly legs. He was also looking pale and a little glassy-eyed. He half fell onto the bed when he reached the bedroom, and she made quick work of feeding the fire in the woodstove so she could get back to him.

She sat on the edge of the bed next to him and helped him out of the suede jacket, draping it over the back of a nearby chair. She pressed the back of her hand to his forehead. He was hot and dry to the touch. "I think you may have a fever."

"It's not a bad one."

She cupped his cheek, not liking the heat rising off his skin. "I'm not so sure."

"I probably just need something to eat." He started to push up off the bed, but she gently pressed him back into the pillows.

"I'll get you something to eat in a minute. Let's check your temperature first." She retrieved the first-aid kit stored in the bathroom medicine cabinet and put the thermometer in his mouth. "We probably need to change your bandage, and I'd rather do that on an empty stomach if you don't mind."

She saw his lips quirk around the thermometer, and she darted him a tentative smile in response. His smile faded, replaced by a furrow in his brow. She sighed and crossed to the window, looking out at the trees beyond the cabin.

She felt his gaze on her, acutely aware of the tension that hung in the air like a heavy mist. The taut silence seeped into her pores, chilling her bone-deep.

She broke the quiet. "I saw a couple of wolves this morning. They're making a comeback here, or so they say. They were beautiful." She turned to look at him. He was watching her, his eyes slightly narrowed.

She crossed to the bed and removed the thermometer. Her heart sank at the reading.

"That bad?" he asked.

"A hundred and two." She shook down the thermometer.

"So give me some aspirin."

She shook her head. "That's not going to be enough." She put the thermometer back in its case and set it on the bedside table. "You need antibiotics."

He pushed himself up in the bed, trying to hide a grimace of pain. "Maybe I just need to eat something. Where'd you put our stash of supplies?"

"In the kitchen." She put her hand on his shoulder as he started to get up. He was scalding hot to the touch. "In a minute. Let me take a look at your wound. Unbutton your shirt."

He unfastened the buttons, his gaze locked with hers. "I'll have to add nursing to your list of known skills."

"I have a list of known skills?"

One corner of his mouth notched upward. "You're a kick-ass poker player."

"Well, that might come in handy when we run out of money," she murmured, helping him shrug the shirt off. She gestured for him to turn his injured side to her. Gingerly, she removed the tape holding the sanitary napkin in place. The pad was heavy with blood, but the bleeding had stopped for now.

"I'm going to have to clean it a bit, but it shouldn't hurt as much as it did last night."

"Easy for you to say."

She ignored the wry comeback and went to the bathroom for a clean washcloth and some antibacterial soap. She returned with the cloth and another sanitary napkin. There were only a couple left in the package. She'd need to find a store nearby and do some shopping sometime today.

She cleaned the dried blood away from the bullet wound, wincing at his soft gasps of pain. "Sorry…sorry."

"Where's the whiskey?" he gritted through clenched teeth. But as she reached for the bottle she'd left on the bedside table, he caught her wrist. "Just joking. I'm okay. Just get it done."

He let go of her wrist and she resumed her cleaning job.

She didn't like the angry red color of the flesh around the torn skin. "I think it's getting infected."

"So put some ointment on it."

She was already pulling the small tube from the first-aid kit, but she shook her head as she dabbed a liberal dollop of the ointment into the open wound. "I don't think it's going to be enough. You need antibiotics."

"That takes a prescription."

"We need to find a doctor, then."

He shook his head. "They have to report gunshot wounds to the cops, and I don't yet know which cops around here I can trust. I'm pretty sure we've already been betrayed once."

She placed the clean sanitary napkin over the wound and taped it in place. "This isn't the kind of thing you can ignore, Joe."

"We can talk about it over breakfast." He shrugged his shirt on again and started to swing his legs over the side of the bed.

"No, you stay here." She stilled him with a touch. "I'll get the food. We have some bread and peanut butter—how about a sandwich? Not much of a breakfast, but—"

"That's fine," he gritted, easing back against the headboard. "Don't suppose this place has a coffeemaker?"

"I don't think you need to drink anything hot, anyway." She released his shoulder. "Might raise your temperature more."

He caught her arm as she started to go, his calloused thumb moving lightly over the soft flesh of her inner wrist. She turned to look at him and was surprised to see a hint of vulnerability in his gray eyes. "I appreciate your worrying about me. I do. But I'm tough. I'll be okay. I'll take some aspirin or something after we eat and the fever will go right down. You'll see."

She didn't bother arguing. She could tell he already had his mind made up. Talk wouldn't make him budge. But she didn't think aspirin or ibuprofen was going to be enough to get his fever down. It had come on too quickly to be anything easily fixed.

She'd just have to take matters into her own hands.

# Chapter Six

The River Lodge Diner's lunch crowd had been brisk, but by one, the bustle of activity had begun to wind down. Only a handful of locals remained at the diner counter, nursing cups of coffee and chatting.

On his stool at the end of the counter, Clint had a ringside seat for the hick-town follies, taking in the latest gossip, from fisticuffs at the local churches to salacious speculation about the new high school football coach and the head majorette.

The pay phone on the wall near the bathrooms rang. The older waitress, Doris, finished filling his cup, set down the coffeepot and went to answer.

Clint could make out only a few words of her end of the conversation—"doctor" and "prescription"—but not much else. However, the furrow in Doris's brow deepened as she talked to whoever was on the other end of the line, piquing his curiosity. He was tempted to feign a trip to the bathroom to get close enough to hear more, but she hung up before he could make a move and returned to the counter to check on the younger waitress's progress.

Boyd Jameson returned from the cashier's desk and

glanced up and down the lunch counter, looking for any errors in the waitresses' work. Doris came back to the counter and poured coffee for a pair of big-rig drivers at the end of the counter.

Jameson made a grumbling noise but the bell over the front door distracted him. "Customers," he barked.

Doris was already untying her apron. "Sorry, Boyd. My shift ended at one. Let Alice get it. She's good with the customers. Here's my ticket pad." Doris handed him the order book and disappeared into the back of the diner, leaving Boyd to bark a terse order at a nervous young waitress, who scurried off to seat the new arrivals.

Boyd looked Clint's way, his scowl disappearing and his game face appearing. "More coffee, sir?"

"I'm good," Clint said, his mind still on Doris and the mysterious phone call. "You know, I was hoping I'd find that dark-haired girl working here today—curly brown hair, freckles, kind of thin—"

"That's Jane. She doesn't work here anymore."

Clint looked at the restaurant manager, contemplating his options. If he was going to find her anytime soon, he needed to start making alliances.

He pulled out his business card and handed it to Jameson. The restaurant manager's eyebrows arched upward.

"Clint Holbrook," he said to Jameson. "Call me Clint. I'm looking for the woman you call Jane Doe. She's wanted for murder in Wyoming and other crimes back East. And I think your friend Doris might know where she is."

Gone to get more supplies. Don't worry—I'll be back.

JOE STARED at Jane's neatly penned note and cursed. He should have handcuffed her to the bed spindles when the thought had first occurred to him.

At least this time she'd left his gun behind, safely tucked into its holster on the bedside table.

He pushed himself to his feet, struggling with a wave of dizziness and nausea. He waited for it to pass before he went to the bathroom.

After relieving himself, he moved to the narrow sink and turned on the tap. He splashed cold water on his hot face and looked up at his reflection in the mirror. His face was ashen, dark circles purpling the skin beneath his bloodshot eyes. He looked as bad as he felt, and that was saying something.

He touched the bandage on his side, wincing as the cloth pulled against the ragged wound. How had he managed to get himself into such a helpless state, forced to depend on the whims of a woman he didn't trust with his dog, much less his life?

He wandered around the bedroom, gritting his teeth against the pain. Pain he could handle. But he couldn't afford weakness. And if he kept lying around here, giving in to the injury, he wouldn't be prepared to deal with whatever danger Jane Doe was about to bring into his life with her latest stunt.

He knew all too well that where Jane went, trouble followed.

JANE SLUMPED in the front seat of the Silverado outside the Fill-Mor gas station on Route Five, trying not to draw attention. She had a long wait; the station was at least an hour from Trinity, and it would take a little while for Doris to get her doctor to call in the antibiotics prescription.

She'd already passed the time by using some of her dwindling cash reserves to stock up on food and first-aid supplies, but after a while, she'd realized she could loiter inside the food mart only so long before people started to notice her.

She didn't like being away from Joe this long. It wasn't likely that he'd sleep the whole time. And while she'd left him a note, she'd been deliberately vague about where she was going. She knew that would worry him. But knowing exactly what she was doing would worry him more.

She closed her eyes a moment and took a couple of deep breaths through her nose to calm her rattled nerves. The scent of leather mingled with another scent—dark, rich, masculine. The smell stirred a memory, the feel of Joe's hands on her face, the touch of his lips on hers, tender yet demanding.

They'd known each other before Idaho, back in a place called Canyon Creek, Wyoming. That kiss the night before had proved that their relationship had been far more complex than she'd previously believed.

But did she really want to know just how complex?

She rubbed her gritty eyes, regretting the sleepless night. Whether she liked it or not, she and Joe were being hunted by a man who'd already proven he was capable of cold-blooded murder. And she suspected he had a big advantage over them.

He knew who she really was.

She closed her eyes against the glare of sunlight reflecting off the plate-glass windows at the front of the food mart, and tried to settle her chaotic mind. For five months, she'd lived second to second, afraid to be still for fear that she'd finally start remembering something. Angie had always found that sentiment strange—not wanting to remember? But Angie didn't live with the bone-deep certainty that her past was something she wanted to escape, not uncover.

Nothing that had happened to her over the past few days had done anything to change her mind about that.

But she couldn't run away anymore. Her past was the danger now. She had to figure out a way to unlock the door to where her memories lay, or she and Joe might not get out of this mess alive.

An image flashed through her mind without warning. A man's face. Not the blue-eyed man she'd seen in her apartment but someone a little older, with thick black hair streaked at the temples with silver. He was handsome, but his dark eyes were shifty and restless, moving constantly.

Full of secrets.

A loud rapping noise jerked her upright. Jane snapped her eyes open, squinting against the glare, and almost wilted with relief when she saw Doris Bradley's warm eyes looking at her through the truck window.

Doris stepped back, giving her room to open the door of the truck. Jane hugged the older woman, grateful for a friendly face. "Thank you so much for this, Doris. I don't know how I'll ever repay you."

Doris handed her the small white bag. Inside, Jane could hear pills rattling. "I wish you could tell me what's going on," Doris said.

"I promise, one day I'll tell you everything." Jane put the bag in the truck and turned back to Doris. "How much did this cost you?"

Doris waved it off. "Not enough to worry yourself about. You're not hurt, are you? Or sick?"

Jane shook her head, averting her gaze from Doris's.

She could see the curious questions in Doris's eyes, but to her relief, the older woman didn't ask them aloud. Jane couldn't have answered them, anyway. She'd already put Doris in enough danger as it was.

Doris gave Jane another swift hug. "Call me if you need anything, okay?"

"I will," Jane said, although she knew she couldn't put Doris in the middle of her mess again. "Listen—you be careful driving back, okay?" *And be careful who you talk to,* she added silently, watching Doris drive away with a sinking heart.

There were so few things in her life that felt familiar or comfortable, and watching one of them drive away felt like the ground shifting beneath her feet.

She climbed into the truck and buckled her seat belt, looking at the pharmacy bag on the seat beside her. She hoped it was worth the effort Doris had made—and the hell she'd catch from Joe when she returned to the cabin.

THE DOOR to the cabin swept open before she even stepped onto the porch. Joe filled the doorway, his hair mussed and his eyes blazing. "I suppose I should be glad you left the gun behind this time."

She stopped on the top step, gauging his mood. Angry but not spitting fire. It could be worse. "Didn't want to leave you unprotected."

He looked at the plastic bags she held in both hands. "Shopping couldn't wait?"

"No," she said seriously. "It couldn't."

He held her gaze for a long moment, his eyes narrowed and dark with tension. Then he stepped back, beckoning her to enter the cabin.

A shudder of awareness tingled through her as she slipped past him in the tight confines of the doorway and entered the great room. He led her to the long leather sofa near the fireplace and sat, his gray gaze watching her as she settled beside him and gave him a quick once-over. He looked pale and feverish, but at least he was awake and relatively alert. She deposited her purchases on the coffee table and reached up to test his temperature.

He caught her hand, trapping it against his face. "You didn't have to sneak out."

Her hand tingled where it lay trapped between his rough palm and his beard-stubbled jaw. "You wouldn't have let me go alone, and you needed your rest."

"I wouldn't have let you go at all," he corrected with a wry grimace. He released her hand, and she dropped it to her lap, curling her fist against the lingering sensation still buzzing through her fingertips.

"Maybe that's why I had to sneak," she murmured.

"Fair enough," he admitted. "Did you get some ibuprofen?"

"Yes. And something better." She reached into one of the plastic bags and retrieved the small paper sack with the bottle of antibiotics. "Amoxicillin. You're not allergic to penicillin or anything like that, are you?"

His brow furrowed, his gray eyes dark with alarm. "Where did you get those?"

"Does it matter?"

He grabbed the bottle and looked at the label. "Doris? Your friend at the diner?"

"She has chronic ear infections—all she has to do is call her doctor and he calls her in a prescription because it happens so often."

"And now she knows where we are."

"No—I met her on Route Five at a gas station. She doesn't know where I went from there."

He raked his fingers through his hair. "You shouldn't have risked it."

She placed her palms on either side of his face, worried at how hot he felt. "You have a high fever. Your wound may be getting infected. I'm not even sure the amoxicillin is going to work, but it was worth the risk to find out. So shut up and take it."

He pressed his lips together, his eyes flashing with irritation, but he opened the prescription bottle and shook out a tablet.

Jane opened a bottle of water and handed it to him. Reading the directions on the label, she said, "You need to take two now, then one in the morning and one in the evening until they're gone."

He added another tablet to his palm and put them in his mouth, washing them down with the water. He wiped his mouth on the back of his hand and met her concerned gaze. "What else did you get?"

"Like I said, I got some ibuprofen, too." She opened the bottle and shook out a couple of caplets. He downed them with the rest of the water and set the empty water bottle on the table.

"I don't suppose you got any real bandages this time, did you?" He picked up one of the plastic bags from the coffee table and started going through the contents.

"As a matter of fact, I did." She took the bag back and

pulled out a box of gauze pads she'd found at the convenience store. "Let's see how that wound is doing."

He followed her to the bedroom, close enough that she could feel the heat of him washing over her back. He sat on the bed and started unbuttoning his shirt, wincing as the movements jarred his injury.

"Easy," she murmured, moving his hands away from the buttons and taking over. Her fingers shook a bit as she finished unbuttoning the shirt, especially with Joe's smoldering gaze fixed on her face.

Heat flooded her cheeks, making them burn, but she focused on keeping her trembling fingers steady enough to guide the buttons through the holes until his shirt lay open, baring his lean, muscular chest and flat stomach.

She stepped back, licking her dry lips. "I think you can take it from there."

The corners of his mouth quirked slightly as he eased out of the shirt and laid it on the bed beside him. He slanted a look at her. "Why'd you come back here?"

The question caught her by surprise. "What?"

His gaze followed her as she pulled the chair up next to his bed and sat. "You had the truck, the cell phones. All the money. You could've left me here and gotten away. Nobody could've stopped you, not for a while."

That he was asking such a question at all made her stomach hurt. "That's what you think of me?"

He didn't answer aloud, but the wariness in his eyes, darkened by something that looked very much like pain, told her the answer to her question. She looked away, sickened.

The image of a dark-haired man flickered through her mind—the same handsome face, same silver-flecked sideburns she'd remembered before when she was waiting outside the food mart for Doris.

*She was watching him, somewhere in the midst of a crowd. She felt small and scared. Scared of him. Scared of what he wanted from her.*

*His green eyes met hers in the crowd and he gave a nod. Her stomach clenched, but she moved forward into the crowd, following his gaze until it settled on a heavy-set man in the front row. The man with the sideburns blinked twice and looked away. She bit her lip and bumped into the heavy man. "Sorry, mister."*

*He spared her a half glance and returned his attention to the dark-haired man and his busy hands as they dealt a new hand of three-card monte. He never felt her small hand slip into his back pocket and remove his wallet.*

"Let's get this bandage changed. Okay?" Joe's voice pulled her out of the memory.

She forced herself into action, trying not to give in to the hot tears pooling behind her eyes as she gathered her supplies and went to work. The redness around the ragged edges of the bullet wound hadn't increased since the last bandage change, to her relief. She cleaned it as gently as she could, reapplied some antibiotic ointment and taped the new gauze in place. "How's that feel?"

"Better," he said, his voice tight. "Thank you."

She couldn't meet his gaze. "You're welcome."

"No, I mean thank you for everything. The antibiotics— that was resourceful. I appreciate the trouble you went to." She still heard anger and distrust in his voice, but apparently he was too much of a straight-shooting cowboy not to express gratitude where gratitude was due.

"I just hope they help," she said.

"Me, too, because we need to get out of here soon."

"I told you, Doris doesn't know where I went."

"All she has to do is let it slip that she saw you at a gas station halfway to here and people will know we didn't keep going to Boise. People know you were Angela Carlyle's roommate. Somebody may even remember she brought you here once. We need to move on as soon as we can."

"Maybe tomorrow. But I want to give the antibiotics some time to work before we try to make another long drive in the truck. Okay?"

He considered her words with a slight frown but nodded. "Okay."

"Good." She stood. "I'll go make soup for dinner. We have chicken noodle and chicken noodle."

"Actually, I think I'd like to have some chicken noodle if that's okay," he said with a half smile that faded quickly. His gaze grew serious and wary, and her heart sank.

"Chicken noodle soup it is," she murmured, heading back to the kitchen before the tears she'd been fighting all day escaped her eyes.

She heated the soup in a saucepan, waiting on a stool at the breakfast bar while it came to a simmer. Angrily knuckling away the tears under her eyes, she thought about her most recent memory. So, a murder suspect, a con artist's henchwoman and now a pickpocket, too.

What other hidden sins would come back to haunt her before this was all over?

# Chapter Seven

Joe watched Jane push the spoon around her bowl of soup without eating and felt guilty about his earlier anger. She'd taken a big risk to get medicine for him, and he had to admit that between the ibuprofen and the antibiotic, he was starting to feel a little stronger.

Which was a good thing, since he'd meant it when he'd told her they needed to leave the cabin as soon as possible, before somebody put the pieces together and figured out where they were.

"We should get out of here tomorrow morning first thing," he told her. "I think we need to figure out how to ditch the truck, too."

She looked up at that. "How're we going to do that?"

"I'm not sure," he admitted. "But whoever put that tracking device on the truck knew you'd be with me."

"Maybe it was Sheriff Trent."

Joe shook his head. He'd considered that, but the Trinity chief of police struck him as a straightforward kind of guy. If he hadn't wanted Joe to get Jane out of there, no questions asked, he'd have said so. "I'm wondering about the man you saw at Angela's apartment."

Her eyes softened in the waning afternoon light. "You believe me."

"There was another witness," he said gruffly, then regretted the tone when he saw the wounded look in her eyes. "And I believe you. About that, anyway."

The wounded look deepened, and he clenched his jaw, hating himself for hurting her and hating her for breaching his fragile trust in the first place. He looked down at his own half-eaten bowl of soup.

"I guess I'd better go pack, then. So we can leave first thing in the morning." She started to push away from the small table, but Joe reached out and caught her hand. Her gaze flickered up to meet his, her green eyes darkening to a mossy hazel.

"Finish your soup," he said, keeping his voice gentle so that it sounded like a request rather than an order.

She looked down at his hand on hers. Color bloomed in her apple cheeks. "I'm really not that hungry—"

He let go of her hand. "Think of it as medicine. You need to keep your strength up. We don't know when we'll get to eat again after we leave tomorrow."

She picked up her spoon, took a bite of soup. "You sound like you've done this before."

"Not this exactly. I've done some cattle drives in the Wyoming Rockies. That can be pretty primitive." Of course, he'd always known he'd end up back home, sooner or later, for hot food and a warm bed. The unknown stretching out before them at the moment lacked that safety net.

Her lips quirked. "Cowboy Joe indeed."

He fumbled the spoon at her soft words. Pain made a fist in his heart and squeezed hard, catching him by surprise.

He felt her gaze on him, but he didn't look up, retrieving his spoon from the table and wiping the soup off the scuffed wood with a paper towel.

"Who was I to you?" Jane's voice was soft. Hesitant.

He made himself meet her wary gaze. "You worked for my brother as his housekeeper. I told you that."

"And that's all?"

He put his spoon on the napkin by his bowl. "We saw each other a few times."

"You mean dated?"

"Yeah."

A dozen emotions darted across her face in the span of a couple of seconds before her expression shuttered. When she spoke, her voice was neutral. "How long?"

"Five months."

Her eyes flickered with surprise. "That long?"

He nodded.

She processed the information quietly, but he could see her doing the math. Five months together meant more than just the occasional dinner and movie outing. More than just holding hands while walking through the park or a goodnight kiss at the door.

But she didn't ask the question aloud, to his relief.

"We'd better finish the soup before it gets cold," she said, bending her head over her own bowl.

He turned his attention to his own soup, aware that the advice he'd given her earlier was even more important for him. He had to keep up his strength, which had already been compromised by the bullet wound and the infection.

But he couldn't help but wonder if he'd ever have enough strength to deal with many more nights alone with Jane Doe.

SHE SLIPPED into the middle of the crowd, catching sight of the dark-haired man. He gave her a quick blink, the signal to sidle up to the mark and put on a show.

He was clearly a tourist, overdressed for the hot, dry climate. He seemed fascinated with the old man's nimble fingers as they shuffled and dealt the cards.

The onlookers were all in on the scam. They played the game, won or lost as needed, and softened up the mark for the kill. Now it was her turn.

"It's the second card," she murmured to the mark.

He looked down at her, surprised.

"Trust me. The queen's the second card," she said.

The dealer took the bets from one of the shills and flipped the cards. The queen was the second card.

The mark looked at her. "How'd you know?"

"He shows you the queen every time, right? Don't watch the queen card. Watch the others."

He frowned at the advice. "That sounds harder than watching the queen."

"Just do it."

The mark turned his attention to the dark-haired man's hands as they switched around the cards. When he stopped, the mark said, "I think it's under the card to his left."

One of the shills who'd placed the bet pointed to the card in the middle. The dark-haired man shook his head and flipped the card to his left instead, revealing the queen. The shill cursed loudly, paid his debt and stomped away.

"You've got it now," she encouraged the mark. "Wanna lend me twenty so I can make a bet? I'll split it with you when we win."

"How 'bout I use the twenty myself and keep it all?"

*the mark responded, pushing his way to the front of the crowd and slapping a twenty-dollar bill on the table.*

*The dark-haired man met her gaze in the crowd and smiled at her. She tried to smile back, but her stomach hurt. She watched the mark lean into the game, his gaze following the cards as the dealer switched them around.*

*The man picked the card to the dealer's right. The dealer flipped it. A seven of hearts.*

*The mark looked over his shoulder at her, contempt blazing in his dark eyes. She saw the dark-haired man give the signal. One of the shills called out, "Cops!"*

*The crowd started to disperse as planned, on cue. She started running as well, heading for the nearest alley, but someone grabbed her from behind. She called out, kicking and screaming, but the others had already scattered. She saw the dark-haired man look her way and pause, briefly, before dashing away.*

*She turned to face her captor. It was the mark, fury darkening his ruddy face. He released her long enough to reach into his pocket and pull out a badge. "Reno Police," he said. "You're under arrest."*

Jane woke with a start, her heart pounding. The nightmare remained in hazy fragments that she struggled to put together. A con game. An undercover cop.

Reno Police.

Whoever she really was, she had an arrest record in Reno, Nevada. It was her first real clue to her true identity—and a stark reminder of just why she hadn't wanted to remember her past.

She shivered as the cold night air curled around her shoulders where the blanket had slipped during the night.

She sat up and wrapped it around her, peering through the darkness to get her bearings in the unfamiliar bedroom.

She felt her way to the door and walked a few feet down the narrow corridor to the bedroom where Joe slept. The woodstove cast a golden glow over the room as well as warmth, lighting the path to the bed where Joe lay. She crossed to the bed, gazing down at his sleeping form. She'd double-dosed him with ibuprofen before bed, knowing he'd need as much rest as possible before they hit the road in the morning.

Now, she knew where to go next. Reno, Nevada.

But this time, she was going alone.

A NOISE STIRRED Joe into consciousness. He lay still, listening for a repeat of whatever had jarred him awake, but he heard only the soft hiss and crackle of the fire in the woodstove.

He was about to drift off to sleep again when he heard a soft, scraping noise from the front of the cabin. Instantly alert, he swung his legs over the side of the bed, ignoring the ache in his side, and pushed to his feet. He left his boots behind, opting for stealth, and grabbed his Colt from the bedside table.

As he stepped into the hallway, he heard the clink of metal on metal—keys rattling, he realized. He crept forward into the darkened great room and saw the front door swing open and a small, thin silhouette start to ease its way through the narrow opening.

He slipped up behind her, catching the door as she started to swing it shut.

Jane whirled around, her face a pale oval in the dim

moonlight. Her wide eyes gazed back at him with a mixture of relief and guilt.

"Just where the hell do you think you're going?" he asked, closing his hand over hers and retrieving his keys from her trembling fingers. "Don't give me any bull about looking for firewood this time."

"Reno," she said, defeat in her voice.

He took a step back, surprised by her answer. "Reno?"

"I had a memory. A dream, really, but I think it was a memory." She leaned against the door frame, her gaze turned toward the truck sitting parked just a few feet from the porch. A distant look came over her moonlit profile. "I was in Reno. Someone will know me in Reno."

He leaned against the opposite side of the door frame, studying her face, trying to figure out what was the truth and what was just another lie. "So you were going to sneak out of here, steal my truck and leave me up here alone?"

She looked down at her feet. "I was going to call Chief Trent to tell him where to find you."

"Am I supposed to thank you for that?"

She looked up at him. "No."

"I would have gone with you to Reno."

"I know you would," she said. "That's why I didn't tell you."

"I don't understand."

Her half smile looked painful. "I know."

"Then explain it," he said, his voice deepening with frustration. He wanted to reach out and shake her, to make her remember everything he needed to know, to make her tell him the truth—the whole truth this time—so he could be rid of her for good. Out of his life, out of his mind, out of his—

What? His heart? He tamped down that idea with brutal force, refusing to dredge up that particular part of their past. Those feelings were dead and buried alongside his brother Tommy. All he had left inside him now was a gnawing hunger for answers.

"I don't know if I can explain—" Jane's words cut off abruptly, and her brow furrowed as she stared into the woods behind him. He turned, following her gaze, and saw what had caught her attention.

Car lights, moving slowly up the winding gravel road toward the cabin.

"Oh, God," she whispered.

He watched for a second to make sure the lights were actually coming toward them. "How much traffic does this area usually see at this time of year?"

"Angie said not a lot. There aren't any cabins between here and the road, and none beyond here." Her voice sounded small and scared, catching him by surprise. To this point, she'd been tough as rawhide, taking on everything thrown at her with pluck and grit. He turned to look at her in the pale glow of moonlight. She looked tiny. Fragile.

The way she'd looked the first day he met her.

He knew better, now. He knew there were more layers to her than just the wounded bird who needed a little tenderness and patience to thrive.

But God help him, she could still get to him in spite of everything.

He touched her cheek. "It's going to be okay."

She put her hand over his. "What are we going to do?"

He pulled her inside the cabin and shut the door, locking it behind them. The flood of adrenaline coursing through his veins started to clear the cobwebs from his sleepy brain. "We have a few minutes. I need you to go to your room, put on extra clothing. Grab anything we can carry on us—matches, snack bars, whatever. I don't know if we're going to have to make a run for it without the truck, but we better be prepared. Got it?"

She nodded and hurried off to the bedroom.

He crossed to the window and moved the curtains aside, peering out at the lights moving closer, and prayed those headlights belonged to a tourist who'd taken a wrong turn.

JANE RETURNED to the great room to find Joe shrugging on his heavy suede jacket. He'd already put on his shirt and boots. She didn't see his gun anywhere, but she knew it had to be within reach.

Outside, the low growl of the car engine continued its inexorable approach. "It's my fault, isn't it?" she murmured. "For calling Doris."

"We don't know that," he answered, even though she could tell he thought she was right. He didn't seem angry about it, though.

The sound of the engine grew louder, then suddenly died. Jane met Joe's gaze, her heart pounding.

The knock on the door made her whole body jerk.

"Shh," he murmured.

"Maybe if we don't answer they'll go away."

"I don't think so," he whispered. "That doesn't sound like a tourist."

The next knock proved him right. "Smith County Sheriff's Department!"

Jane tried to calm her racing heart.

Joe looked at her. "Two tourists, vacationing in the mountains," he whispered. "That's all we are."

"Why don't you flash your badge and tell 'em to butt out of your investigation?"

He grinned a little at that. "That'll be plan B." He flicked on the light and crossed to the door as their visitors knocked a third time.

He opened the door a crack. "What is it?"

"Smith County Sheriff's Department. May we come in?"

"Can I see your identification?" Joe asked.

Jane heard a rustle of movement and caught a flash of metal in the narrow opening of the doorway.

Joe looked the badges over carefully for a moment, then stepped back. "How can I help you?"

Two deputies in tan uniforms stepped inside the cabin. The taller of the two tipped his hat at Jane. "I'm Deputy Lowell. This is Deputy Garland."

A nervous bubble of laughter caught in Jane's throat at the polite introduction, so at odds with the terrified tension that had her wrapped up in knots.

"We've had a citizen issue a complaint against a Mrs. Sarah Holbrook, and he told us we could find her here." Garland, the shorter deputy, looked pointedly at Jane.

"I don't know any Sarah Holbrook," she blurted.

"Neither do I," Joe agreed. "What sort of complaint?"

"Armed robbery. He said Mrs. Holbrook pulled a knife on him and stole his car and several thousand dollars in cash." Garland took a step toward Jane. "What's your name, ma'am?"

"Jane," she answered.

"Last name?"

Jane looked at Joe. He gave a little nod, and she answered, "Doe."

Garland's eyebrow ticked upward.

"She has amnesia," Joe said.

Both Garland and Lowell stiffened at his words. Garland's hand dropped to his hip holster as he exchanged a look with his partner.

"I'm going to have to ask you to put your hands up against the wall, ma'am," Garland said, motioning toward the wall by the fireplace.

"What's this about?" Joe asked, taking a step forward. Lowell put out his arm, blocking him. Joe turned toward the deputy, his face flushed with anger. "You don't know what you're doing here. This woman is not who you're looking for."

"How do you know? You said she had amnesia," Lowell responded, drawing his weapon.

Joe held up his hands. "I'm a cop, that's why. Let me get my identification out of my pocket."

"That won't be necessary," a new voice interrupted from the doorway.

Jane's body stiffened at the familiar tone, her heart lurching to a stop before skittering into hyperdrive. She forced her gaze upward.

A tall, sandy-haired man in a black overcoat moved unhurriedly into the cabin, his gaze seeking Jane's. He locked eyes with her, a slow, satisfied smile creeping over his full lips as he saw that she recognized him.

"Hello, Sarah," he said.

He was clean-shaven and well-dressed now, but she'd remember those cold blue eyes till the day she died.

He was the man who'd killed Angie.

# Chapter Eight

Joe looked from the newcomer to Jane, taking in the look of horror on her face. The hair on the back of his neck rose. "Would someone like to tell me what the hell's going on?"

"Mr. Holbrook, you were supposed to wait in the car," Deputy Garland gave the man a stern look, but Holbrook didn't even look at him. His gaze remained fixed on Jane's pale face.

Joe stepped between Jane and Holbrook, blocking her from his view. "Who's Sarah?" he asked.

Holbrook looked at him through narrowed eyes. "This woman. My wife. I'm Clint Holbrook, Sarah's husband." His voice softened. "She's not a stable woman. You realize that, don't you?"

"That's enough, Mr. Holbrook." Deputy Lowell moved in close, taking Joe's arm. "Sir, we're taking Mrs. Holbrook in for questioning. I'm afraid we'll have to ask you to come in with us, as well."

"On what charge?"

"Right now, it's just for questioning," Garland answered in a soothing tone Joe knew well. It only served to irritate him.

"I'm a policeman. I know how this works, and I want to know what this man told you to get you out here in the middle of the night instead of waiting until morning." And how had he found them? Had Jane's friend Doris spilled the beans?

"Sarah has already shown herself to be a flight risk," Holbrook answered smoothly. "Haven't you, darling?"

Joe felt the heat of Jane's body as she moved up behind him. She curled her fingers in the back of his shirt, just above where his Colt nestled in the waistband of his jeans.

"He's the one who killed Angie," she said, her voice low and strangled.

Joe looked up at Holbrook, trying to square him with the description Jane had given to Hank Trent. Add a beard, mustache and a baseball cap, put him in all-black clothing—

"My wife is delusional, Mr.—?" Holbrook paused, waiting for Joe to supply his name.

Joe didn't bite, pretty sure that Holbrook, whoever he was, already knew Joe's name and probably a whole lot more about him. He turned to the two deputies. "Mr. Holbrook is wanted in Trinity, Idaho, for questioning in a murder."

Garland and Lowell exchanged glances. "He told us you'd say that."

"I'm afraid the man has been infected by my wife's paranoia." Holbrook's voice was tinged with a hint of sadness. He met Joe's gaze, a triumphant light burning in the blue depths of his eyes. "You see, she's a very sick woman. Paranoid schizophrenia. She needs to be in a hospital, not in a cabin in the wilderness."

Jane's fingers tightened their grip on Joe's shirt.

"I suppose you have proof of what you're saying?" Joe asked, fairly sure the man would produce papers to support his statement. Clint Holbrook looked like the kind of man who tied up all his loose ends.

"Of course. I've shown them to the deputies."

"We don't want a mess here," Lowell said, looking warily from Joe to Clint Holbrook.

"We can't go with them." Jane's voice trembled. He felt her scoot closer to him.

The two deputies exchanged a look, and Joe realized how out of proportion Jane's fear probably seemed to them. It made her seem irrational. They probably thought he was just as irrational for indulging her fears.

They were wrong. He had a gouge in his side to prove it. And he'd seen Angela Carlyle's body. Jane couldn't have slit her throat that way, but Clint Holbrook could've.

Proving it, however, was another matter altogether. And in the meantime, there were two suspicious sheriff's deputies looking for a reason to truss him up like a turkey and run him in.

He turned to Jane. "We have to do this." He tried to communicate calm through his gaze and in the tone of his voice, but the panic in her eyes remained. "The deputies will help us sort things out."

Jane's expression hardened to a cold mask. "Nobody can help me," she murmured. Her voice sounded distant, as if she weren't even here in the room with him anymore. It sent another shudder rippling down his spine.

Suddenly, she wheeled and ran for the back of the cabin, catching everyone by surprise. Joe started after her, but behind him, Holbrook shouted, "Gun!"

Someone hit Joe from behind, slamming him into the

cabin wall. He gasped as pain rocketed through his injured side, robbing him of breath. He felt an arm press against his neck, pushing his face into the wall.

"Don't you move!" Deputy Lowell growled in his ear. He reached under Joe's shirt and pulled the Colt from his waistband, laying it on the side table next to them.

"I told you I'm a cop!" Joe protested.

"Just hold still—"

Joe heard Jane cry out from the back of the cabin. "Jane!" he called, his own panic starting to rise. Where was Holbrook? Was he back there with her?

Joe tried to turn his head to locate the man, but Lowell pushed his face back into the wall. "I said hold still!"

"She tried to bite me!" Garland's indignant voice rang out in the hallway, followed by the sounds of a struggle.

"Jane!" Joe called out, needing to hear her answer.

"Touching, your concern for my wife," Holbrook murmured, his voice close.

Joe stopped resisting Lowell as cold anger swamped him, driving out the worst of the panic. "Deputy, it's bad procedure to try to make an arrest with civilians in the line of fire."

"He's right, Mr. Holbrook," Lowell said. "You should've stayed in the car."

"If it will make things easier…" Holbrook's footsteps retreated.

Joe heard the cabin door open and close. He waited a moment, then asked the deputy, "Is he gone?"

"Yeah."

"Listen, I realize you have every reason to believe that guy. But he's lying to you. He is a suspect in a brutal murder in Trinity, Idaho—"

"I've seen the BOLO on that murder," Lowell said, referring to the Be On The Lookout message Sheriff Trent had issued to surrounding law-enforcement agencies. "It was for a guy with a beard."

"It was a disguise!" Joe pressed his forehead against the wall. "I helped write the damned thing, so I know it said the guy might be wearing a false beard. Look, just let me go and I can explain exactly what's going on—"

Lowell eased his forearm away from the back of Joe's neck but held on to his arms. He slapped a cuff over one of Joe's wrists.

"What are you—" Joe ended the question on a breathless profanity as the deputy started pulling his other arm into place to fasten the cuffs, stretching the ravaged skin over his gunshot wound.

"He's hurt!" Jane cried out from across the room. "That bastard out there shot him. Don't do that!"

Lowell stopped pulling on his arms and lifted the left side of his shirt. Cool air washed over Joe's side, making the skin pucker.

"Holbrook shot you? Did you see him do it?"

"We didn't see the shooter," Joe admitted.

"It was him," Jane insisted.

Joe turned his head to look at her. Garland had her hands cuffed behind her, and the struggle had mussed her hair and clothes, but otherwise she looked okay. She met his gaze, her eyes wide and scared but her chin high with determination.

"You saw him, then?" Lowell asked her as he pulled Joe around and clamped the cuff over his wrists in the front.

"She didn't see him, either," Joe answered before she could speak the lie he saw forming in her eyes. "But she did see him in the apartment where her friend was murdered."

"So she says." Garland nudged her forward.

"I believe her," Joe insisted.

"Well, maybe you're being straight with us, and maybe you're not, but we can sort that out when we get back to the station." Lowell gave Joe a little push. "Let's go."

The night air was bitterly cold, sliding under the collar of Joe's shirt and racing down his spine. Lowell thrust Joe's suede jacket into his cuffed hands when they reached the sheriff's cruiser. "Hold on to that for me."

He turned to unlock the backseat of the car. Joe saw the deputy's service weapon snapped tightly into his hip holster, in easy reach. Slipshod. He'd have ripped his own underlings a new one if he'd seen them being so lax.

A moment later, he realized his own weapon was nowhere in sight. "What did you do with my Colt?" he asked.

Lowell turned to look at him. "What?"

A bark of gunfire shattered the quiet woods, and Lowell's whole body jerked and spun, going down.

Something small and solid rammed into Joe from behind, pitching him against the car door as he tried to see what direction the fire was coming from. He heard a soft whimper—Jane—and then Deputy Garland shoved them both aside, unlocking the front door of the cruiser with one hand while trying to draw his weapon with the other.

A second gunshot cracked in the middle of the commotion. Garland grunted, his fingers clutching the car door. It swung open as he tumbled away and hit the ground with a thud.

Joe crouched behind the car door and looked over at the

fallen deputies. Head shots, he realized with a sinking heart as he took in the damage. They were both dead.

With his hands cuffed, he couldn't reach behind him to touch Jane, but he felt her huddled close. At least his body was shielding hers.

"Get into the cruiser," he growled at her, moving to give her an opening while he scanned the darkness in front of them. "And stay low."

While she scrambled into the front seat and curled into a knot in the passenger side floorboard, he threw the jacket in the car, then retrieved the deputy's car keys from the ground and tucked them into his shirt pocket. He finally spotted movement as Clint Holbrook stepped into the opening, aiming Joe's own Colt M1911 pistol at the door providing Joe with his only cover.

Adrenaline pumping like fire in his veins, Joe dropped and scrambled for the nearest deputy's body, tugging the service pistol from the deputy's hip holster. He whipped it up and didn't take time to aim through the narrow space between the door and the cruiser's chassis. He just snapped off a couple of rounds and threw himself into the cruiser's driver's seat, pulling the cruiser's keys from his pocket.

Ignoring the howl of pain racing up and down his injured side, he twisted his body to turn the ignition key. The cruiser roared to life, the headlights slicing through the dark night. They lit up Clint Holbrook like a spotlight, making the man squint.

It wasn't much of an advantage, but Joe did what he could to make the most of it, gritting his teeth against the agony as he twisted his body twice more, first to pull the car door shut and then to put the car into gear.

He hit the gas and went straight at Holbrook, forcing

the man to dive toward Joe's truck to avoid being rammed. Holbrook jerked the truck door open and took cover behind it, lifting his gun toward the cruiser.

The deputy's vehicle probably had a bulletproof wind-shield, but Joe didn't want to risk finding out. Growling through the pain, he turned his body to reach the gearshift again and slammed the cruiser in Reverse.

There was limited space to get between the deputies' bodies and the dark sedan parked behind and to one side of where the cruiser had originally been, but Joe gripped the wheel and gave it a shot. The passenger side of the cruiser caught the sedan's side mirror, bending it a bit and making a loud scraping noise as they passed, but they made it through the gap and onto the gravel drive.

Joe didn't have time to do more than glance out the window to see what Holbrook was doing. He saw the man make a run for the sedan, firing the Colt as he ran. A thud hit the side of the cruiser. Jane made a soft mewling noise that made Joe's heart drop like a rock.

"Jane, are you hit?"

"No. Just go!"

He spun the steering wheel, reversing the direction of the cruiser, and shifted to Drive. He gunned the engine, making the cruiser shimmy across the loose gravel a few seconds before he righted it and headed down the mountain road with the pedal to the floor.

He knew he had a good jump on Holbrook, but he didn't let up until they reached the main highway. He kept an eye on the rearview mirror for signs that Holbrook had caught up with them, but he saw nothing.

Still, he remembered the GPS tracker from before. Holbrook had been outside with the cars for a while. He couldn't assume the man hadn't put a tracker on the cruiser as well, in case one or both of the deputies had managed to escape his assault.

"Jane, you can get up in the seat now."

She pushed herself up to the passenger seat, meeting his quick gaze with wide, frightened eyes. "The deputies?"

He shook his head.

She uttered a soft curse. "Are you hurt?"

He felt blood oozing down his injured side, but he didn't think it was serious. "I'm okay. You?"

"A little bruised up, I think, but not bad." She wriggled a little in the seat. "Damn it, why didn't they cuff me in front, too?"

"How limber are you?" he asked.

She gave him a look. "I've never had to find out."

"If you can manage to get your hands in front of you, there might be an extra handcuff key in the glove compartment."

He forced himself to keep his eye on the darkened highway ahead, though the soft grunts and noises Jane was making tempted his gaze in her direction more than once. After a couple of minutes he heard her release a deep sigh and a soft, triumphant "Yeah!"

He glanced at her and saw she now had her hands in front of her. "Good girl," he said quietly.

She rooted through the glove compartment, spilling some papers and a flashlight into the floorboard before she emerged with a paper clip. "No key, but maybe we can make this work."

She pulled the coils of the paper clip open, twisting the flexible wire into a modified L shape with a small downward bend at the tip.

Joe pulled the cruiser over onto the shoulder of the highway and put it in Park, looking at the bent paper clip in her hand. He released a soft laugh.

She looked up at him, her eyebrows quirked. "What?"

"I should've known you'd know how to shape a handcuff lock pick."

She looked down at the clip, her expression crestfallen. "I didn't even realize—"

"It's okay. Can you see if you can unlock me?" He held out his cuffed wrists.

She made quick work of the lock, tears sparkling on her eyelashes as the lock sprung and he pulled off the cuffs. He took the lock pick from her and released her hands, as well. She rubbed her wrists and lowered her head. "Now what?"

"Stay here while I check something." He got out of the cruiser, shrugged on his jacket and circled the cruiser until he was certain there was no GPS tracking device attached to the underside of the chassis. The cruiser itself would probably have an internal device the sheriff's department could track through its own system, but Clint Holbrook would have to go through channels to get access to that.

As he got into the cruiser, he heard the radio on the dashboard squawk. A male voice—dispatch, he guessed—asked for a ten-twenty from unit four.

Jane cleared her throat. "I think that's us. You better answer."

He started to reach for the radio, then stopped. "If I don't answer, they'll come looking for us."

"I know, so answer it."

He looked at her. "Those deputies deserve to be found before the wolves you saw get to their bodies. I'm not going to answer and pretend I'm them."

"It'll buy us time."

"I said no."

She pressed her lips to a thin line, but he saw understanding in her eyes, battling with her need to get away from the danger. She gave a quick nod. "But now we're going to have to ditch the cruiser. And soon."

"I know," he said. But it would take a while for the sheriff's department to figure out what was going on. That bought them a little time to get rid of the cruiser and find another way out of the area.

THEY LEFT the highway after a few more miles, weaving their way south down county roads and back roads so lightly traveled they ran into no other traffic for a solid hour.

Jane buckled her seat belt and settled back against the passenger seat, turning her head so she could watch Joe's profile as he drove. His brow was creased, probably with pain. She saw him drop his left hand to his side more than once.

"Are you bleeding again?"

"A little. Not much."

Jane fell silent, trying to clear from her mind the image of the fallen deputies. She made herself picture Clint Holbrook instead, studying the lines of his face, the color of his hair and eyes, trying to place him in the dark chasm that hid her lost memories.

He'd told the deputies and Joe that she was a paranoid schizophrenic. But that couldn't be true, could it? She'd lived for five months in Trinity without anyone thinking her insane, hadn't she? And she'd known Joe and his brother before that, and Joe didn't act like she was crazy, either.

"Did you believe him?" she blurted aloud.

Joe slanted a look at her. "Holbrook?"

"Yeah. Did you believe what he said about me?"

Joe's hands tightened on the steering wheel. "I don't know. You were keeping secrets when I knew you. I guess maybe you're his wife. I don't know."

"No, I mean about the other thing."

He frowned, as if uncertain what she was asking. Then his brow straightened, and his lips curved in a half smile. "That you're a paranoid schizophrenic?" He released a huff of laughter. "No. You're as sane as I am."

Surprised by how relieved his reassurances made her feel, she cleared her throat. "But what if he tells his story to Chief Trent? What if he explains away his presence at Angie's apartment and turns it all back on me?"

"Trent knows what the evidence says. The person who killed Angela had to be a lot bigger and stronger than you. I don't think Holbrook will try to sell that to the Trinity cops," Joe assured her.

She hoped he was right.

"Listen, we need to ditch this cruiser, and soon. That means risking the highway again so we can find a truck stop or something. Maybe a no-tell motel that won't ask too many questions if we show up on foot without luggage."

"Any idea where we are right now?"

"We just passed into Boise County, heading west."

"We can take Highway 21 into Boise, but that's probably a good three hours from here. I think there are truck stops along that highway, and probably a few cheap places to stay where people won't ask a lot of questions. I can't tell you exactly where, though."

"Then we'll just drive until we find one," he said.

## Chapter Nine

The Shamrock Motel sat, low-slung and shabby, just off Highway 21 about two hours outside Boise. Its Las Vegas-style marquee was missing several lights so that the sign read ham ock in neon green.

They came upon it less than a mile down the road from the Lucky 21 Truck Stop, a fact that combined with Joe's growing exhaustion to overcome his dismay at the motel's seedy appearance. Back up the highway about a quarter mile, he'd spotted a turnoff that might provide them a good place to hide the cruiser. As soon as he could find a place to turn around, he reversed course and backtracked to the turnoff, driving down a winding gravel road for another quarter mile until he found a stand of trees that would hide the cruiser from view, at least until full daylight the next day. By then, he planned to be already at the truck stop, looking to grab a ride on a big rig into Boise.

Joe pulled the dead deputy's service weapon out of the waistband of his jeans and laid it on the car seat. He saw Jane's curious sidelong glance. "We'll get further unarmed," he explained. "Less conspicuous."

She nodded.

They cut through the woods, keeping the highway in sight, until they reached the clearing where the Shamrock Motel sprawled under the blue-green combination of the waxing moon and the anemic neon of its marquee sign. Joe told Jane to wait in the parking lot while he went inside and rented a room for the night.

The desk clerk took his money without really looking at him, no doubt aware that the less he noticed, the fewer questions he'd have to answer when someone with a badge or a P.I. license inevitably came calling. Joe signed the register "Mr. and Mrs. John Clark" and the clerk handed him the key to room 24.

Jane followed him to the room, located at the far end of the motel. There were only a couple of other cars in the parking lot, and no signs of occupation down where their room was located.

Jane went immediately to the bathroom as soon as they got inside, leaving Joe to drop wearily onto the bed, hoping the worn bedspread was relatively clean. He was surprised to see a phone on the bedside table; a lot of places like the Shamrock Motel didn't bother with that sort of amenity, knowing its typical clientele wouldn't require more than a bed and relative anonymity.

He picked up the phone and dialed the operator. Asking to place a collect call, he gave the operator the number of his deputy chief's office in Canyon Creek and prayed that Riley Patterson was pulling one of his usual late nights.

His second in command answered on the second ring. The operator told him there was a collect call from a Sheriff John Clark and would he accept the charges? Joe held his breath, hoping his old friend would remember their games of Cowboys and Indians from their childhood days.

"I'll accept," Riley said.

Joe released his pent-up breath.

"Joe?" Riley asked when the operator left the line.

"Yeah, it's me."

"Are you okay?" The worry in Riley's voice caught Joe by surprise.

"I'm okay. Listen, I don't have long—"

"Neither do I. I just got a call from an FBI agent out of the Idaho Falls Resident Agency. Did you know you're wanted for murdering a couple of Idaho cops?"

Joe closed his eyes, his head hurting. How had Holbrook managed to set up the frame so quickly? "I can explain—"

"Don't call me here again." Riley hung up on him.

Joe stared at the phone, dumbfounded. What the hell was going on? He knew Riley. Had known him his whole life. There was no way he would have bought any story about Joe being a cop killer.

The phone to the police station was already being monitored, Joe realized. Riley had forced him off the line before they could finish a direct trace.

It would buy them a little time, although whoever was trying to discover their whereabouts would eventually follow their tracks to the Shamrock Motel. With luck, it wouldn't happen until they were already headed west to Boise and the relative anonymity of the bigger city.

But Joe couldn't risk calling Riley or his office again. He was effectively cut off from all the people he could trust.

He and Jane were on their own.

"Jane?" He looked around the empty motel room. The door to the bathroom was closed.

She'd been in there a long time, he realized. Too long.

Pushing to his feet, he crossed to the door. "Jane?" he called, his gut tightening with alarm. Had she been hurt in the ambush and hidden it from him? Had she climbed out the bathroom window and run away?

He heard soft snuffling sounds inside, which relieved him on one count but scared him on another. He tried the door handle. It was unlocked.

"Jane, I'm coming in." He pushed the door open.

Jane looked up at him from the floor, where she sat huddled on a towel between the tub and the toilet. She'd stripped off her clothes and thrown them in the tub, leaving her shivering in her underwear. Tears reddened her eyes and stained her face. "I didn't want you to see me like this," she said, wiping her cheeks with the back of her hand.

He crouched in front of her, wincing as his injured side protested. "Like what? Human?"

She managed a watery laugh before her expression fell. Her lips trembled and fresh tears spilled from her eyes. "I'm so tired of having other people's blood all over me."

"I know." He thumbed away her tears, cupping her cheek in his palm. "Tell you what. Let's get you under the covers and warmed up, and I'll see what I can do about getting the blood out of your clothes before morning."

She let him pull her to her feet. As he started to turn away, she lifted her hand to his face, her palm rasping against his beard stubble. "You're feeling a little feverish."

"We'll have to find some ibuprofen in the morning before we head to Boise."

Her eyes glittered with pride. "No, we won't." She picked up something sitting on the edge of the sink and put it in his hand. It was a small, clear, resealable plastic bag full of pills. "Ibuprofen and your antibiotics. I had them in the pocket of my jeans."

"Smart girl." He took out one of each and dry-swallowed them, then tucked the bag in the pocket of his own jeans. He pulled a relatively clean-looking towel from the rack by the tub and wrapped it around Jane. "Let's get you into bed."

"I bet you say that to all the pathetic, sniveling girls," she murmured as they left the bathroom.

He chuckled, but deep down, a ribbon of pain threaded through his heart. She sounded so much like the Sandra he remembered, the wounded, beautiful creature who'd turned his life upside down at a time when he hadn't believed he could ever care about a woman again. She'd gotten under his skin so easily it was frightening, with her combination of vulnerability and steely strength. She was doing it again, chipping away at his armor piece by piece, and he didn't know what to do to stop it.

He didn't even know if he wanted to anymore.

"NINETY-FOUR DOLLARS and seventy-eight cents." Jane slid the last penny into the pile in front of her and looked at Joe with a sinking heart. "We need more cash."

He nodded. "I think I can get us a ride to Boise with a trucker at the truck stop up the road. But when we get there, we're going to have to find an ATM and get some more cash."

"You can't do that! They'll be looking for you."

"I know." He scooped up the money and put it back in his wallet. "But they'll be expecting us to end up in Boise anyway, right? We can use that to our advantage." He settled back against the headboard, pressing his hand against his left side as if he was in pain.

She scooted up the bed to sit beside him, reaching for his shirt to check the wound. "Is it still bleeding?"

He let her look, lifting his arm and settling it over her shoulders. A shudder of pure, feminine awareness rippled through her, but she forced herself to concentrate on his injury.

The bandage she'd put in place back at the cabin hours ago had held, but blood had seeped through to the surface. "I wish we had some way to change the bandage, but there's nothing sterile in this place."

"There's a shop at the truck stop. I noticed it when we passed. We can probably pick up a few things there," he said, his breath gently hitting her ear.

She lifted her head and found his face inches from hers. The air between them crackled with tension. His arm felt heavy on her shoulders, his fingers curling around her upper arm and pulling her closer.

Heat washed over her, swamping her with yearning. But as she felt herself leaning toward him, a flash of memory pushed through her desire-fogged brain. The angry undercover cop, his face red and his eyes dark with satisfaction.

*Reno Police. You're under arrest.*

She pulled back, sliding away from his arm. "We should go to Reno, Nevada."

THE BUS TRIP from Boise to Reno took over twenty hours. Despite the discomfort from his wounded side, Joe had settled down to sleep an hour out of Boise, suggesting she do the same. They'd gotten very little sleep in the past forty-eight hours, and they didn't know what would await them in Nevada.

But Jane remained wide-awake, even as they crossed into Utah several hours later. Despite the whirlwind of activity that had started with catching a ride with a big-rig trucker from the Lucky 21 Truck Stop and ended with a mad dash to catch the bus to Reno, Jane couldn't settle down so easily.

They'd hit the ground running in Boise, searching out a couple of different cash machines so Joe could max out the cash advances on his credit card. He'd also used a credit card to book them two one-way tickets to Portland, Oregon, to throw people who might be tracking his credit-card purchases off their trail.

They'd used some of the five thousand dollars in cash at a nearby drugstore and another cheap motel, where they'd changed their appearances—a buzz cut for Joe and red hair dye for Jane. They'd picked up cheap backpacks and some supplies and clothing at a discount store near the bus station, using another couple of hundred dollars from their cash supply. By 10:30 a.m. they'd bought two one-way tickets to Reno, also with cash, and boarded the bus for the long, winding trip to Nevada.

Even though she was exhausted, Jane couldn't stop worrying about what waited for her in Reno. For all she knew, she'd been there just once, gotten arrested, and that was the end of it. There was a part of her that wanted to find nothing in Nevada to link her to her past. Every instinct she had was screaming for her to run away and put her past—whatever it might be—behind her.

But her past wasn't going to leave her alone. Clint Holbrook, whoever he had been to her, wasn't going away.

He'd called her his wife. But she didn't feel like his wife. She felt no sense of connection to him, only a deep, grasping fear and a fast-growing hatred for all he'd done to hurt the people she cared about.

She glanced at Joe sleeping beside her. Without the Stetson to hide his new buzz cut, he looked more like a soldier returning from a hard war than a cowboy cop.

He also looked pale and a little thin. They hadn't eaten much over the past couple of days, and the infection, though proving mild enough for the amoxicillin to handle, had taken a toll on him. She hated waking him when they reached Salt Lake City, but they had to transfer buses. She shook his shoulder, trying to be gentle, but he started awake, his eyes wild with the surge of adrenaline.

He relaxed a bit as he took in their surroundings. "We're in Salt Lake already?"

She nodded. "We have a long layover. How about we get something to eat?"

They joined the throng of travelers exiting the bus at the Salt Lake City station, Joe keeping her close by draping his arm over her shoulders. They'd agreed on a cover story for their travels—newlyweds on an economy honeymoon. They even wore a pair of stainless-steel wedding bands they'd picked up cheaply at the discount store in Boise.

She toyed with the ring as they left the bus station, staying close to Joe. Outside, Salt Lake City sparkled like a thousand jewels as twilight descended. The setting sun painted the mountains in the east in tones of gold and red, reminding Jane of the Sawtooth Mountains back home.

Her stomach twisted as that word rang in her head. *Home.* That's how she'd come to think of Trinity, but only because she knew nothing else but those five short months there. That time was the sum total of life as she knew it.

For better or worse, it was time to leave Trinity behind and find out who she really was.

Joe caught her hand as they crossed the street, following the crowd toward a large mall visible a few blocks ahead. They found a sub sandwich shop in the mall and grabbed a couple of sandwiches for dinner. Jane enjoyed the anonymity of the large mall, the sense of safety in numbers. As they ate, she found herself pretending she was just an ordinary woman, having dinner with a friend.

A boyfriend, she amended mentally. Since it was her fantasy.

Maybe they had met in college. Joe was probably a few years older than she was, but maybe he'd worked a while and gone to college later. He'd majored in criminal justice, of course. Top of his class. Her major had been—

What? What interested her? What was she good at? She had no idea.

"What did I tell you about myself? Back in Wyoming," she asked aloud.

Joe looked up from his dinner. "Not much, really. You didn't talk about your past. You were all about the present. And sometimes the future."

"Did I tell you other things about myself? What my dreams were? What talents or skills I had?"

He gazed across the table at her, his expression apologetic. "Not a lot. I know you liked music. You could play the piano."

"I play the piano?" She smiled at that.

"Yeah. You said you came to it later in your life and wished you had been able to take lessons when you were younger. You wanted to be better at it."

"Did I ever play for you?"

His expression softened. "Yeah. You did. I have a piano at home. It belonged to my mother, but she died before she could teach me to play. My father thought piano lessons were a waste. I was going to be a rancher like he was, and that was that."

"But you're a policeman instead."

He nodded. "Call me a rebel."

She laughed. "Oh, yeah. You're a rebel."

He smiled. "You used to tease me about that."

"About what? Being a rebel?"

"Being a cowboy. Mom, America, apple pie—"

"Cowboy Joe," she murmured.

"Yeah." His smile faded, and she could almost see him putting deliberate distance between them. "Let's see if we can find a clothing store around here anywhere. We need a few more things if we're going to spend too much more time on the move."

They spent the next hour looking for a few items to add to their stash of supplies. Joe bought a gym bag to accommodate the jeans and fleece items they bought in case they had to rough it outdoors. They were a couple of months from temperate weather, especially at night. "It won't hurt to be prepared," Joe said as they took the last of their supplies to the checkout stand.

They made it back to the bus terminal with a half hour to spare. During the wait to board the new bus, Joe transferred their purchases to the gym bag, while Jane counted up what cash they had left. "We still have about $2,000," she told him softly.

"Maybe that'll be enough," he answered.

"Enough for what?"

"To make more," he answered cryptically.

The boarding call came before she could ask him what he meant. He picked up the extra bag, gave her a look. "Reno, here we come."

She followed him slowly to the bus, terrified of what lay ahead.

## Chapter Ten

"Double down, mister," Joe said to the blackjack dealer, taking Jane's hand and kissing it "for luck" as he'd explained to the dealer the first time he'd done it. Jane slanted a look at Joe, amused by the relish with which he was playing the role of the clueless bumpkin for the blackjack dealer.

The dealer arched an eyebrow, looking at the three and the seven in his own hand. Joe held a nine and a two. The dealer laid down another card for Joe. A three of hearts.

Jane flashed a friendly smile at the blackjack dealer, a man in his late fifties who looked like a permanent fixture behind the table. He was older than the dealers she'd talked to at the other casinos.

The Painted Pony Casino was the third they'd tried since heading for the strip early that morning. They'd come up empty at the first two. Nobody admitted to knowing the con man Jane had seen in her dream.

Maybe she'd get lucky here.

"I've always thought it would be fun to be a dealer," she commented airily. "Do you have to know any math?"

The dealer looked up at her with an amused smile. "Can you add up to twenty-one, ma'am?"

"Yes."

"That's all the math we want to see going on at a black-jack table," he answered, dealing himself a card. The six of clubs. He glanced up at Joe, who was lightly drumming his fingers on the blackjack table. "Newlyweds?"

Joe gave Jane a look so besotted that it made her stomach turn flips. "Just got hitched," he answered with a sly wink at the dealer. "Now I've got to make a little money to pay the bills."

The dealer uncovered the facedown card in front of Joe—the six of diamonds. He played his own facedown card. A jack of spades. "I guess it's your lucky day all around, then, mister." He slid the winnings toward Joe.

"I used to come to Reno with my family when I was a kid," Jane said as Joe motioned for the dealer to deal him another hand. "I can barely remember any of it. There was this guy though—an older guy. I remember he had coal-black hair with just a little gray at the temples. And he dealt that game—what's that game where there are three cards, and you switch them around and around and someone tries to guess where the queen or the ace or whatever is?"

"Three-card monte, darling," Joe drawled, tapping the eight of hearts in front of him. "I don't think folks here at the casinos consider that a proper card game."

The dealer grinned as he dealt Joe a queen of diamonds. "No, we don't. And, ma'am, if you run into that particular guy again, turn around and run the other way."

A flutter of excitement rippled through Jane, tinged with apprehension. She darted a look at Joe. He fingered the edge of his card and tried to look more interested in the game than the conversation.

She couldn't be quite so nonchalant about their first lead all day. "So you know the guy I'm talking about? Does he ever come here to the Painted Pony?"

"If it's the guy I'm thinking about, he still runs those games now and then, but he hasn't been welcome in any legitimate casino in town in years."

Joe laid the back of his hand against Jane's cheek. "Baby, you're not going to drag me off to some shell game just so you can take a trip down memory lane, are you?"

She pouted. "You promised for better or for worse."

Joe shook his head at the dealer. "Women."

"Do you know the guy's name? Or even where we could find him?" Jane asked, ignoring Joe's exaggerated sigh.

"His name is Dugan. Harold or Hal or something like that." The dealer lowered his voice as a couple of men in suits passed. "There's this poker palace down on Pridemore called the Lady Luck. Supposedly just a bar, but everybody knows there're backroom games going on for the patrons no longer welcome in the casinos. Dugan's a regular."

"Gee, thanks," Joe drawled.

"Hard to say no to a lovely lady," the dealer said with a shrug and a wink at Jane. He laid another card on Joe's hand. A three of clubs.

Joe grinned. "I'll stay."

The dealer's smile was halfhearted. He dealt himself a queen, which put him over twenty-one. "A winner again." He pushed the chips toward Joe. "Another hand?"

"Actually, I promised my wife we wouldn't spend all day in the casinos. But thank you very much for the games." Joe rose, pocketing most of the chips but leaving a generous tip for the dealer.

"Thanks on behalf of the employees," the dealer said with a nod. "Hope you enjoy your stay in Reno."

Joe tucked his arm around Jane's waist and guided her toward the cashier's booth to cash in his chips. "You're quite the little storyteller, aren't you?" he murmured, his lips brushing the tip of her ear. A spark of pure electricity zigzagged through her at the light touch.

"Got us the information we were looking for," she replied softly.

"If it's the same guy," Joe warned.

The cashier took the chips and started handing Joe cash. Jane watched her count out the bills, her eyes widening with surprise. He had won over $3,000 at the blackjack table.

"I get the feeling you've gambled before," she murmured as they stepped into the midday sunlight outside the casino and started west toward their motel.

He gave her a considering look, dropping his arm from her waist. He faced forward, quickening his pace. "I don't make a habit of it."

Jane hurried to stay in step. "Took guts to double down with the dealer holding ten."

He glanced at her. "How would you know?"

She stumbled to a halt, considering the question. "I have no idea."

He paused and looked back at her, a little frown creasing his brow. He released a soft sigh and motioned with his head. "Come on. Let's get back to the hotel. I could use a rest before we go looking for your con man."

She caught up with him, putting her hand on his arm. "I'm sorry—I'm pushing you too hard."

He looked faintly horrified by the notion. "I'm fine. But we haven't had a lot of sleep in the past few days."

She couldn't hold back a soft chuckle. "Well, it helps to sell our newlywed cover story."

He slanted a look at her, his lips curved with a half grin that made her heart skip a beat.

The Admiral Arms Motel was a couple of blocks off the strip, within walking distance of several of the town's casinos. It hadn't been exactly cheap, and they'd taken one of the last rooms available, but the room had been clean, with a pair of double beds. They'd even managed a few hours of uninterrupted sleep before rising early to start their tour of the casinos in search of information.

Of course, the easiest way to find out who she really was would have been to head for the Reno Police Department, let them take her fingerprints and check them against their records. But she couldn't risk it. What if she was wanted for more than being a con man's shill?

She hadn't told Joe everything about her dream, only the memory of the con man and the certainty that she had known him here in Reno, although the more she thought about it, the sillier she felt about being so reticent. He already suspected her of complicity in his brother's murder. What was fraud compared to that?

Joe grabbed the phone book as soon as they got back to the room, sitting on the edge of the bed to thumb through the listings. "Well, what do you know? There's no Lady Luck listed in the phone book."

Jane sat across from him on the other bed. She picked up the phone, drawing a small frown from Joe. She dialed the number for the front desk.

A woman picked up. "Admiral Arms Motel."

"I'm trying to find a particular establishment in the

phone book and I'm having no luck. A business associate asked me to meet him there later this evening. It's a tavern called the Lady Luck, on Pridemore, but I'm not familiar with that part of town. Have you ever heard of the place?"

There was a brief pause before the clerk answered. "I've heard of it. I'm sorry, I don't know the phone number, but we do have city maps available for sale at the front desk if you'd like to pick one up. It will show you where Pridemore Avenue is."

"Thank you. I'll do that." Jane hung up.

"No luck?"

"Well, it exists. And it's on Pridemore Avenue, I think. And going by the tone of her voice, the desk clerk thinks I'm nuts even to consider going there." She pushed her fingers through her hair, scraping it back from her face. "I'm hungry. Are you hungry?"

"A little."

She pushed off the bed. "Give me a ten and I'll run down the strip to one of the burger joints for us."

He stood, as well. "I'll come with you."

"Don't be silly. You rest. I'll be back in a flash."

"You're not going anywhere without me."

She stared at him in growing dismay. "You mean you don't trust me to go anywhere without you."

He shook his head. "I mean I don't like the idea of you out there by yourself with someone gunning for us. We're safer together."

He was right, she knew, but she wasn't sure he was telling her the whole truth, either. Clearly, he didn't trust her, and who could blame him? A woman with a hidden past, a dangerous present and an uncertain future? She wasn't even sure she trusted herself. What if her past came rushing back to her while she was out there alone? What would she remember? What might she do?

She nodded finally, conceding his point. "Okay. You're right. Together it is."

She followed him out of the motel room.

JOE AND Jane bought a couple of burgers and shared an order of fries at one of the fast-food joints not far from the motel. At midday, the temperature was nearing seventy degrees, warm enough for Jane to suggest they eat their meal at one of the outdoor tables.

"Have you ever been to Reno before?" Jane asked Joe.

He shook his head. "Some buddies and I took a trip to Vegas once, during spring holiday, but not Reno."

"I think I like Idaho better. Closer to the mountains."

He finished his hamburger and wadded up the paper wrapper, spinning it between his fingers on the concrete table in front of him. "I went to college in Texas," he said, smiling at the memory of his four years in College Station. "Hot as hell from March until October, and flat as a pancake. I missed the Rockies."

"I wonder how long I lived here in Reno." Her green-eyed gaze swept over the street scene in front of the hamburger joint as if seeking something familiar.

"What do you remember? Besides just being here, I mean," he added when she turned to look at him.

"Not much," she admitted. "A street scene. The black-haired man playing three-card monte."

"What makes you think this man can tell you anything about yourself?"

She sighed, bending a thin French fry between her restless fingers. "I'm pretty sure I worked for him."

The confession shouldn't have surprised him. God knew he'd thought much worse things of her. But her soft admission made his heart sink. "Worked for him how?"

"In one memory I had, I picked a man's pocket on his cue." Her gaze skittered away from his, her face flushed. "And in a later dream, I was talking a mark into a shell game the man was running."

"How do you know these memories are real?"

She plucked at the bun of her half-eaten hamburger. "I guess I wasn't sure. Not until we talked to that blackjack dealer and he knew the man I was describing."

"Do you know how old you were then?"

"I don't even know how old I am now." She looked up suddenly, an eager light in her eyes. "Do you?"

"I'm not sure," he admitted. "You told me you were twenty-five when we first met. That was almost a year ago. But I don't know—"

"You don't know if I was telling the truth," she finished for him. She looked down at her sandwich for a moment, then folded it in its wrapping paper and stuck it back in the paper bag where they'd put their trash. "Why don't we head back to the motel and get a little rest?"

He caught her hand, stilling her movements as she started to stand. "It probably wasn't a lie," he told her. "You're probably twenty-six."

"But you don't know," she said sadly. "You don't know that anything I told you was the truth, do you?"

He couldn't deny it.

She slipped her hand away from his, picked up the bag of trash and put it in the nearest trash bin. He had to hurry to catch up with her, falling into stride as she reached the sidewalk. "Do you want me to lie to you and tell you I think everything you said was the truth, even what I know were lies?"

She halted, turning to look at him, her eyes narrowed against the bright sun. "No. Of course not. I'm not angry at you. I'm angry at myself. Or whoever it was I used to be." She sighed, pressing her fingertips to her forehead as if trying to rub away a headache.

He touched her arm, making her look at him. "Let's just go back to the motel and rest a little while. A nap will do us both some good."

She didn't move, even as he gestured for her to join him in resuming their walk back to the motel. He stopped after a couple of steps and turned back to her.

"Do you still think I killed your brother?" she asked.

The question caught him by surprise. He'd had exclusive, private access to her for a couple of days now, and the subject of his brother's murder had barely come up in all that time.

Did he even think of her as a suspect anymore? Had he ever, really?

Her expression betrayed both fear and hope. "Do you?"

"No," he admitted. "I don't think you killed Tommy."

She released a soft breath, her eyes fluttering closed for a second.

"But you know who did," he added.

Her eyes snapped open. "So do you. Clint Holbrook."

He nodded. "I think so. I think you may have seen it happen."

"I saw it happen?" She looked queasy. "How did he die?"

"He was shot." Joe closed his eyes, trying not to remember the images of his brother's murder scene. "If Clint knows you saw it, it could be why he came after you."

"He could have killed me in the apartment. He could have killed me at the cabin. But he didn't."

Joe nodded. "I'd like to know why he didn't. Wouldn't you?"

She looked away, her gaze turning toward the mountains to the west of the city. "I don't know," she admitted. "He wants me enough to kill people to get to me. That doesn't speak well of me, no matter how you slice it."

He brushed a piece of hair away from her cheek and tucked it behind her ear, his breath catching when she turned to him, her lips parted and a question in her eyes. He dropped his hand to his side. "If you don't want to go to the Lady Luck tonight, we don't have to."

She sighed. "No. We should go." She started walking again, her pace quick and determined.

He followed, his own pace less hurried, his strides just quick enough to keep her from moving too far ahead.

She was right about one thing. Clint Holbrook wanted her enough to kill people to get to her, including his brother. And until they figured out why, neither one of them would be safe.

"SO, YOU WERE counting cards, weren't you?" As they reached the motel parking lot, Jane broke the silence they'd maintained for most of their walk back to the motel.

Joe shot her a look as they started up the stairs to the second floor. "That would be wrong."

She grinned at the flicker of amusement in his eyes. "One day in Reno and Cowboy Joe loses all his ethics."

"Not all of 'em—" He pulled to an abrupt stop as they reached the second floor, catching Jane off guard. She stumbled into him, grabbing his shoulder.

His arm swept back, keeping her tucked behind him. "Can I help you?" he said to someone hidden from her view. Curious, Jane craned her neck to see around Joe's broad shoulders.

Standing in front of the door to their room was the dark-haired man from her memory flashes. His hair was still long and thick, swept back from his wide forehead in a lush black mane. The silver at his temples had spread to the rest of his hair, streaking the black with liberal strands of white, but there was no doubt he was the man she'd worked for as a shill.

He caught sight of Jane and for a second, his expression reflected a hint of surprise and something a bit darker. But he recovered quickly, greeting them with a nod. "Actually, I think maybe I can help you. The name's Harlan Dugan. I hear you're lookin' for me."

Joe stepped forward carefully, keeping Jane tucked safely behind him. "Looking for you?"

Jane pulled away from Joe's grasp. "Do you know me?"

For a second, the man's expression shifted, revealing surprise. But his mask of calm confidence quickly returned. "I can tell you that," he said with a broad smile. "For a price."

*"It's a price you're not gonna want to pay, Harlan!"* The booming voice rattled the Airstream's screen door, making her jump. She looked up in alarm.

*"I can have the whole thing for you by tomorrow morning. Guaranteed."* Harlan's voice carried through the hot desert air as surely as it carried through a gathered crowd on a Reno back street. *"Just give me till tomorrow."*

*The desperation in his voice made her stomach coil into an anxious knot. She looked away from the Airstream, blinking against the afterimage of the sun's hot glare on the trailer's silver side, and picked up the walnut shell she'd dropped.*

"What kind of price?" Joe asked the man blocking the path to their motel room door, jerking Jane's mind back to the present.

"That can be negotiated," Harlan said, looking at Jane. He smiled again. "The red hair is new."

She touched her choppy bob. "It's normally brown."

"I remember." Faint affection glittered in his eyes. "You used to wear it braided all the time."

"So you really do know me."

His brow furrowed. "What happened to you, girl?"

"I don't remember."

"Amnesia?"

"Can you tell her who she is or not?" Joe growled.

Jane caught his arm, squeezing. He looked at her.

"There's always a price," she said, shivering despite the desert sun warming her face.

"I've known people like you," Joe said, contempt in his voice. "I've put them all in jail. The Reno police might be interested in your little extortion scheme—"

"Can you risk it?" Harlan countered coolly. "How do you know she's not wanted by the Reno police? Since she can't remember who she is."

Jane let go of Joe's arm and looked away, another memory dancing just out of reach.

"What's the price?" Joe asked with a sigh.

"I understand you had some success at the casinos," Harlan said. "About three grand's worth."

"Go to hell," Joe said, putting his arm around Jane and starting to go around Harlan Dugan.

"Are you sure you want to risk it?" Harlan asked.

Joe stopped within a foot of him. He towered over Harlan Dugan, who was only a couple of inches taller than Jane herself. "What do you mean by that?"

"Someone's looking for her, am I right?" Harlan looked around Joe, meeting Jane's eyes. "Someone I don't think you want to find you."

Joe grabbed the front of Harlan's shirt. "Stop it with the games, old man."

*"I'm tired of your games, old man!" A giant of a man, burly and bald, burst through the screen door and strode outside the Airstream trailer, his snakeskin boots thudding against the hard-packed soil a few feet from where she sat, legs crossed, practicing with the walnut shells.*

*She tucked her knees up to her chin, ducking her head as he turned to yell at Harlan, who stood in the doorway. "Two grand by tomorrow at noon!"*

*The bald man straddled his dusty motorcycle, revving the engine for effect, and drove off, kicking up a cloud of dust behind him.*

*She looked up as Harlan stepped outside, scratching the side of his neck in a nervous gesture she knew meant bad news. He crossed to where she sat. She could smell his fear mingling with the odor of tobacco smoke and sweat. "Come on, kitten. We gotta go to work now."*

*"Do I have to?" she asked, her stomach hurting.*

Jane jerked her head up and looked at Harlan Dugan, realization dawning. He met her gaze, his eyes narrowing as he realized the game was over.

"Tell her who she is," Joe warned him, his fingers still curled in the front of Harlan's shirt.

"I'm his daughter," Jane said.

## Chapter Eleven

Joe stepped back, releasing Harlan Dugan's shirt. He looked at Jane, his expression tinged with both surprise and concern. "His daughter?"

"So you remember me now?" Harlan asked, his face an impenetrable mask.

"Not entirely," she said. "Just enough to know you used me as your shill from the time I was a child."

"People always fall for the kids," Harlan said with a faint smile. "And you were good, kitten. Real good. You were a natural with a story."

Jane looked away, her stomach roiling. Joe's hand settled in the middle of her back, but she drew away, not wanting him to touch her right now.

Harlan looked at the motel room door. "Reckon we could go inside and have a little sit-down? I'm not as young as I used to be, and all this standing around is bad on my knees."

Jane looked at Joe. He seemed reluctant, but after a brief pause, he unlocked the motel room door and ushered Jane and her father inside.

Harlan took a seat at the small table by the window, leaving Jane and Joe to sit on the edge of the nearer bed.

"This place is nicer on the inside than it looks on the outside," Harlan commented. He reached into his pocket and pulled out a pack of cigarettes. "You mind?"

"Yes," Jane said firmly, the phantom smell of tobacco lingering with her, making her stomach churn even more.

Harlan put the half-empty pack back in his breast pocket and drummed his fingers on the table. "Why were you looking for me?"

"What's her name?" Joe asked.

Harlan looked at him. "Who are you, anyway?"

"He's a friend," Jane said firmly.

Harlan looked around the motel room, taking in the signs of obvious cohabitation. "Should I be saving up to pay for the wedding?"

"Just tell her what her name is." Joe's voice was low and tight, the look in his eyes deadly.

"Shannon," Harlan answered after a short pause. "Shannon Erica Dugan. Born on Valentine's Day twenty-six years ago."

So she was twenty-six, just as she'd told Joe. Good to know there was something she hadn't lied about. "What about my mother?" she asked. "Where's she?"

"Buried next to her mama in Gallup, New Mexico. She didn't stop bleeding after you were born."

Joe touched her again, his hand warm against her spine. This time she let it stay, needing the feel of him beside her just to stay upright. She struggled against a powerful, unanticipated sense of loss. "How long has it been since you saw me?" she asked, her voice strangled.

"About eight years. You hit the road once you were legal and never looked back."

"Did I leave with someone?"

Harlan's eyes narrowed. "I suppose there was a fellow. Isn't there always?"

"But you never met him?" Joe asked.

"No. I suppose I'm not the sort of daddy a girl would want to take a boy home to meet."

"Ever heard of a man named Clint Holbrook?" Joe's hand pressed more firmly against Jane's back as he asked the question she'd been dreading.

"No," Harlan answered quickly. Too quickly. He rose to his feet. "I think you had the right idea, kitten. You were smart to get outta here the first time. You'd be smart to do it again. The sooner the better."

"That's it? That's all you've got to say to your daughter?" Joe stood to face Harlan, his body radiating with anger. "God, you're a piece of work."

Harlan ignored him, leveling his dark gaze with Jane's. His voice held an urgency that made Jane's nerves hum. "Get outta town. You hear me? There's nothing here for you anymore. Take the next plane out of here and go have yourself a nice life."

Jane stood, her knees wobbly. She caught Joe's hand as he took a step forward. "You know who Clint Holbrook is," she said to Harlan. "I need you to tell me everything you know about him."

Harlan paused with his hand on the knob. He turned to look at her, letting his gaze linger as if imprinting her in his memory. "Good luck, kitten," he said.

He opened the door and left.

Joe took a step toward the door, as if to follow him, but Jane caught his hand. "No. Let him go."

Joe threaded his fingers through hers, crouching to look her in the eyes. "I'm sorry…Shannon."

She shook her head, tightening her fingers around his. "I'm not Shannon Dugan. Not anymore. Please don't call me that, okay?"

He lifted his other hand to tuck a lock of hair behind her ear. "What do you want me to call you?"

She lifted her chin and met his gaze. "Jane. Just call me Jane."

CLINT HOLBROOK glanced at the display panel on his ringing phone. Arching one eyebrow at the name, he pushed Receive. "Holbrook."

"You were right. She showed up." Harlan Dugan's voice was tinny and hesitant through the phone receiver.

"Where is she?"

"I don't know. She found me at the Lady Luck. She wouldn't tell me where she's staying."

Clint could tell the man was lying. His lips curved in a half smile. Who would have figured the old bunko artist would have some residual affection for his daughter?

"She said she was heading out of town soon. I tried to get her to tell me where she was going next, but she doesn't trust me," Dugan added.

"Not a problem," Clint assured him, thinking through his next options.

"You're still gonna pay me the five grand, right?"

Clint smiled again, finding pleasure in knowing once again a man's price. "Of course. My associates will be in touch." He rang off and dialed another number.

A deep voice answered. "Gibb."

"I have a job for you," Clint said. "I need you to deliver $5,000 in cash to Harlan Dugan. You will find him at the

Lady Luck Tavern tonight after seven. Please give him the money and a message from me."

Quietly, deliberately, he told Gibb exactly what message he wanted delivered to Harlan Dugan.

"I GUESS that didn't quite go as you expected," Joe drawled softly from somewhere behind her.

Jane's lips curved in a grim smile. "Actually, it did." She let the curtains drop and turned to face him, her eyes adjusting slowly to the darker room. "It went exactly as I expected."

He patted the mattress next to him. She hesitated a moment, her instincts leaning heavily toward isolation rather than comfort. But finally she crossed to the bed and sat beside him.

He took her hand and enfolded it in his own. "I'm sorry your mother's dead."

"And that my father's a self-centered bastard?"

"That, too."

She rested her temple against his shoulder. "When I first realized I didn't know anything about my past, I imagined all sorts of scenarios to fill in the blanks. My parents were professors. Doctors. Spies." She chuckled bleakly. "But I knew better. Deep down, I knew."

"Have you remembered anything else?"

"Nothing new. But there's something I didn't tell you about my earlier memories." She withdrew her hand and shifted on the bed to face him.

He returned her gaze, his expression wary.

"The reason I remembered Reno at all was because I remember being arrested by an undercover Reno police officer," she said. "For my part in Harlan's shell game."

His expression softened. "You must have been a kid,"

he said. "We didn't get any hits on your fingerprints until you showed up in Trinity, but maybe a closed juvenile record wouldn't have been in the system."

"If I left here at eighteen, I guess I didn't have time to rack up a record as an adult."

"You probably never got arrested again, since you didn't show up anywhere on our search." He brushed the back of his knuckles against her cheek. "But we have a name now to help us find out more about who you are."

"I don't want to know who I was."

He cupped her chin in his palm and turned her to look at him. "You can't run away from it, Jane, or you'll spend the rest of your life running."

"I wish I could," she murmured, her heart racing as his fingertips traced the curve of her cheek. "I wish I could keep running until I found a place that feels safe."

"Running away from Wyoming didn't make you safe." His voice dipped lower.

She closed her eyes, unable to think with him sitting so close. "Tell me how we met."

"Tommy introduced us."

She waited for him to withdraw, the way he always did when he mentioned his brother. But she still felt the heat of his body next to hers, the warmth of his breath stirring her hair and warming her cheeks.

With her eyes still closed, she turned her face toward him. "Tell me how. Where were we? What did you say? What did I say?"

His breathing quickened. "All I remember," he whispered, "is wanting to do this."

His mouth brushed over hers, soft and hot.

She opened her eyes, startled. For a brief moment, she

was too surprised to react. By the time that moment passed, any thought of pulling away disappeared.

She parted her lips, returning the gentle pressure, and curled her fingers into the crisp cotton of his shirt to pull him closer. He cradled her face in both hands, slanting his mouth over hers with greater urgency.

Blistering need scorched through her at his touch, catching her off guard. Entangled by desire so fierce she couldn't catch her breath, she fought for control, as frightened by what she was feeling as she was enthralled.

This was memory, she realized, as much as instinct. She remembered these sensations, the feel of his hands as they traced a path of sexual heat down the side of her neck to the curve of her breasts. She remembered the taste of him—rich, dark and bittersweet.

He shifted on the bed and she followed, ending up on his lap, her thighs straddling his hips to bring their bodies flush and hard against each other. Threading his fingers through her hair, he broke off their kiss and made her look at him. "If we do this, I won't be able to let you go," he warned, his gray eyes dark with hunger.

*"I won't let you go." Clint's voice was hard, full of warning. His grip on her wrist tightened, just short of painful. "You know that."*

*He released her and she forced herself not to rub her wrist where he'd touched her. She couldn't let him see her distress. He enjoyed it too much.*

*She tightened her hands into fists and watched him leave the room. The sound of the lock clicking into position was loud in the silence of her bedroom prison. She dropped wearily onto the side of her bed, pressing her hands against her roiling stomach.*

*She had to get out tonight. Before he found out.*

Jane pulled away from Joe's arms, stumbling a little as she slid off his lap and took a few steps away from him. Her heart raced from a double dose of desire and fear.

Joe stared at her from his seat on the edge of the bed, his eyes dark with frustration. "Guess that's a no?"

"I'm sorry," she murmured, edging past him toward the bathroom. She shut herself inside and stared at her reflection in the bathroom mirror.

*Gazing back at her was a person she barely recognized as herself, a well-dressed woman with long, dark hair twisted in a coil at the base of her neck and light but perfectly applied makeup. The only thing familiar was the hunted look in her green eyes and the determined set of her mouth.*

*She had to get out of there.*

*The night was dark, which served her purpose. Miguel had risked everything by providing the code for the back gate. She couldn't let him down by getting caught.*

*Outside, the air was cool and dry, with a faint salt breeze coming from the Pacific a few blocks west. Clint had gone to a party—something political, she thought, though he'd long since stopped informing her of the details of his comings and goings.*

*It would be her last chance to get away before...what? Why was tonight the night she had to leave? She knew the answer was there somewhere, in her fuzzy head, but she just couldn't pull it out.*

Jane blinked and the image in the mirror was gone, replaced by the bottle redhead with tired, sad eyes.

Everything she needed to know about herself lay hidden somewhere behind those eyes. She couldn't run from her memories. They would follow her wherever she went, daring her to suck up her courage and face them.

A knock on the bathroom door made her whole body jerk. She steadied herself with both hands on the sink counter.

"Jane, are you okay?"

"I'm fine," she lied, staring at the mirror as if she could will another memory into being. But her other self remained stubbornly elusive.

She turned on the faucet and splashed water on her hot face, wishing she could return to the moment when all she wanted in the world was to be in Joe Garrison's arms.

But how could she offer herself to him when she didn't even know what she was offering? What kind of woman was she, really? Why was Clint Holbrook willing to kill to take her home with him? Joe couldn't give her those answers. And until she knew the truth about herself, the last thing she could afford to do was give her heart to a man who might never be able to trust her.

SOMETHING HAD to give, Joe thought, staring bleakly at the closed bathroom door. He wasn't the kind of man who sat around waiting for things to happen.

He made things happen.

What he needed was home-field advantage. He knew every inch of Canyon Creek, Wyoming. And more important, there were people in Canyon Creek who'd known him since birth, who knew the kind of man he was and what he was—and wasn't—capable of doing.

He needed to go home.

But getting there undetected was the hard part. His earlier call to his deputy chief—and Riley's quick ring off—had made it clear the authorities were watching his friends and associates. His credit cards were probably flagged, too. Another long bus ride seemed the best option, but it left them at the mercy of the driver and other passengers.

He was tired of being at anyone else's mercy.

The bathroom door opened, and Jane walked into the bedroom, carrying first-aid supplies and a plastic garbage bag she'd apparently taken from the bathroom trash can. She slanted a wary look at him. "Time to change your bandage."

The last thing he trusted himself to do at the moment was take off his shirt. But the unadulterated challenge in her eyes left him with no option. He tugged the hem of his T-shirt upward, wincing as it snagged on the surgical tape holding his bandage in place.

Jane laid her supplies on the bed beside him and helped him slide the shirt over his head. He felt her hands trembling but her expression was all business. She sat by him on the bed, keeping a careful distance. He didn't know whether to laugh or feel insulted.

"I'm sorry," she murmured as she removed his bandage, taking pains to be gentle. "About what happened before."

He wasn't sure if she was apologizing for the kiss or for cutting it short. He went with the former. "It's my fault. You were trying to make sense of what your father had told you and I…changed the subject."

She smiled wryly and tossed the soiled bandage into the plastic bag. "You weren't exactly alone in that."

"Maybe we should talk about that, too."

"I know we had a relationship before, but I don't remember it," she said quietly as she dabbed at his healing wound with some antiseptic wash.

He winced. "I know."

She looked at him. "You don't trust me anymore."

"I don't trust anybody," he admitted, regretting the words as soon as they spilled from his lips.

Her eyes narrowed. "Why not?"

"Forget it."

She pressed her lips together, clearly not happy about letting such a cryptic remark go unexplained, though she remained quiet as she finished cleaning the wound. But as she squeezed some antibiotic cream onto a soft sterile pad, she broke the silence. "Did someone hurt you?"

A bubble of bleak laughter rose in his throat. "You never could just let things go."

She met his gaze. "You told me before?"

"Yeah," he said, old, bitter pain settling deep in his chest. As reluctant as she'd been to share the mysteries of her hidden past, she'd been a bulldog when it came to wheedling his secrets out of him. She'd made him want to share his pain, to let her help him bury it in the past.

"I'm sorry I don't remember," she whispered.

He closed his eyes, trying to resist the pull of her. It was stronger than ever, despite all the lies he'd uncovered since her disappearance.

"Was it a woman?"

"Please, Jane—let it go."

"I must have seemed just like them. Running off, leaving you with more questions than answers."

"You *were* just like them," he said, more bitterly than he'd intended.

She fell silent. He opened his eyes and saw that she was sitting hunched beside him, her cheeks damp with tears.

Something inside him cracked and spilled. "You and I are more alike than you know," he said.

She slanted a look at him, knuckling away her tears.

"I lost my mother when I was a baby, too," he said when she remained silent. "She died in a car accident, leaving my father to raise me."

"I'm sorry."

"I guess I had it pretty good compared to what your father did to you."

"Was your father a cowboy like you?" she asked with a slight smile.

"He owned a ranch."

"Did he raise you by himself?"

"Mostly. When I was two, he remarried. For a while."

She reached for the gauze pad on the bed next to her and resumed bandaging his side, a sideways glance inviting him to continue talking.

"Her name was Melissa. She was beautiful and sweet. She's the only mother I really remember, you know? My own mother was just pictures in an album. Melissa was real."

Jane smiled. "Someone to tend your scrapes when you fell down and hug you when you cried?"

He nodded. "I loved her."

"What happened?"

"My father was a difficult man to love. And life on a ranch is hard. There's a lot of isolation. Melissa was a woman who needed to be around other people. She wasn't cut out for life on the ranch, and my father would have died before moving into town. So she left. And she took my little brother with her."

"Tommy?"

"Yeah." He smiled. "He was four when she left. I was seven. She changed their names back to her maiden name and moved a couple of towns over. That's why his last name was Blake."

"I wondered." Jane laid her hand on his arm. "That must have been so confusing for you."

He sighed. "I got over it. I found Tommy later, when we were both grown. They'd moved back to Canyon Creek while I was away at college. We had some time together before—"

When he couldn't bring himself to say the words, Jane's fingers tightened on his arm. "I wish I could remember what happened that night. I honestly do."

For the first time in a long time, he believed her.

"Did your father ever try to find your brother?"

"No." He'd never forgiven the old man for that, especially when he'd discovered how easy it was to find Tommy when he was old enough to do it himself. "He died while I was in college. I found Tommy on my own. He was right there in Canyon County, working on a ranch in Addison. He was a born rancher."

"And you weren't?"

"I knew I wanted to be a policeman the first time I rode in a cruiser, lights flashing and siren blaring."

Her smile carved dimples into her freckled cheeks. "Were you in the front seat or the back?"

He laughed. "It was a ride-along for career day at my elementary school. When I came home babbling about wanting to be a policeman, my father threatened to have my teacher and the Canyon Creek Chief of Police fired."

"What happened to the ranch after your father died?"

"I deeded it over to Tommy. It always should have been his. Now it belongs to Melissa, as far as I know."

"As far as you know?"

"Melissa and I don't talk. We haven't been on good terms since she walked out when I was seven." He sat upright suddenly, a thought popping into his head. "Every-body in Canyon Creek knows that. Which is why nobody's monitoring her phone, waiting for me to call."

Jane met his excited gaze. He saw her quick mind putting two and two together.

"I think I know how to get us safely home," he said.

# Chapter Twelve

"Joe?" Melissa Blake's soft voice registered surprise and just a hint of wariness. "Are you all right?"

Joe hadn't prepared himself for the rush of emotion that washed over him at the sound of his stepmother's voice. They hadn't talked since Tommy's funeral—the first time in over twenty-five years—and even then, it had been a quick, awkward exchange, both of them too wrapped up in grief and anger to meet each other halfway.

"Joe?"

He swallowed the painful lump in his throat. "I'm fine, Melissa."

A long pause on her end made him wonder if she'd hung up on him. But she spoke finally, her voice thick with emotion. "I've been so worried about you. You know what the news is saying about you—"

"It's a lie."

"I know it's a lie," she said firmly. "The news is also saying you were shot."

"Just a graze. Listen, I don't have much time." He looked across at Jane, who sat on the opposite bed, her anxious gaze fixed on his face. "I need to get back to Wyoming, but I don't want to risk taking public transportation."

"I can send you money to rent a car or something—"

"Thank you," he said, touched by the offer, "but I'd have to show ID and a credit card. I can't risk that, either. I need you to meet me here and rent the car for me. Do you think you can get away without notice?"

"When and where?" she asked without hesitation.

He swallowed hard and looked at Jane. "I need you to take the first flight you can find to Reno. Tonight."

"Reno? Tonight?"

"I'm sorry—I know it's an imposition—"

"I'll be there. Let me arrange it and I'll call you right back with the flight information. Is this the number you want me to use?"

"Yes." He'd called her on the disposable cell phone he'd bought when they'd first hit town. He had a couple hundred minutes to burn—surely enough to get them back to Wyoming safely. "I'll wait for your call."

He rang off and looked at Jane. "She agreed."

"I heard. Was that hard?"

He found the sympathy in Jane's eyes as unnerving as his phone call with his estranged stepmother. He looked away from her, pressing the heels of his hands against his gritty eyes. Was he ever going to get a decent night's sleep again? Weariness was fogging his brain, weakening him.

He'd spent the past year shoring up the defenses Jane had dismantled during the few months of their relationship. That she'd knocked down years' worth of emotional walls so quickly had come as a shock the first time around. That she was starting to knock them all down again, after all she'd put him through, scared the hell out of him.

His cell phone rang, giving him a start. He looked at Jane. She licked her lips and glanced down at the phone.

He answered. "Hello?"

"It's me," Melissa said. "I found an afternoon flight out of Jackson Hole. I can make it, no problem. The flight arrives around ten o'clock at the Reno airport."

"Got it. Listen—you need to pack some food in your bag. I don't want you to have to leave your room until you check out the next day. Take enough to get you through."

Melissa paused. "Do you think I could be in danger?"

"I'm trying to make sure you aren't," he replied. "Thanks for this, Melissa."

"I'm just glad you've given me a chance to repay you," she said, her voice dark with tears. "I'll never forgive myself for being too cowardly to stay and fight for you."

Joe tamped down the emotions her words evoked, trying to stay focused on the present. He and Jane needed to spend the afternoon resting up for the long drive back to Wyoming. He couldn't afford to wallow in old regrets.

"When does she arrive?" Jane asked after he hung up.

"Ten." He stretched out atop the motel bed. "Better try to get a long nap, or we'll fall asleep at the wheel."

She lay facing him, her eyes wide with apprehension. "Are you sure you want to take me back there with you?"

He turned to face her. "It's why I went to Idaho in the first place."

Her eyes narrowed slightly. "That seems so long ago."

"Five days."

"Is that all?"

He nodded, his eyelids drooping. Rolling onto his back, he let them shut. "Get some sleep," he murmured.

Her soft sigh was the last thing he heard as he drifted off.

CRAMPS, *low in her belly.*

*A rain-washed scene viewed through the metronomic swish-swish of windshield wipers.*

*Fear and dread, deep and paralyzing, slowing the world to a terrifying crawl.*

*The world around her went dark and hazy, disjointed sounds and images that she couldn't piece together into a coherent whole. Someone asked her name and she said, "Sandra." But that wasn't her name. Not anymore.*

*She'd left Sandra behind in Wyoming, along with the last of her hope. And Joe.*

*The thought of him brought fresh pain, deeper and broader even than the cramping in her abdomen. She needed Joe. Where was he?*

*She lay swaddled in agony, the world around her disappearing in a haze of pain and fear. She called Joe's name and a soft female voice answered, offering to call him for her. But she shook her head, closing her eyes and her mind to everything that was happening.*

Jane woke with a start, her heart racing. She pressed her hand to her aching chest and tried to grab the disappearing fragments of memory. She had a sense of pain. Fear. She strained for more but nothing connected into any sort of narrative she could make sense of.

In the other bed, a snuffling sound drew her attention. Joe lay asleep, his breathing slow and steady. She stared at him, overwhelmed with a fierce, unfamiliar sense of joy. For a moment, she'd had the terrible sense that he was gone from her forever, but the sight of him drove out the fear, leaving her weak and trembling with relief. She slid off the bed and made it halfway across the space between them before she stopped herself.

What was she going to do? Crawl into bed with him?

She sank onto the edge of her bed and watched him sleep, slowing her breathing to match his. Her pulse calmed in response, approaching normal. But she knew that sleep was now out of the question.

Pushing to her feet, she crossed to the window. Afternoon had begun to creep into evening, the desert sun dipping toward the Sierra Nevada range west of town. Jane watched the shadows on the rough-hewn mountains deepen, creases and folds appearing out of nowhere as if the crags were aging before her eyes.

She checked her watch. Almost five. Five hours to go before they had to meet Joe's stepmother at the airport.

Then home to Wyoming.

She smiled bleakly at the thought. Home.

If you judged such a concept by family connections, she was already home. Her father still lived here in Reno, had apparently done so for at least eight years and maybe more. Put down roots.

And she was leaving here without asking the questions that only her father could answer.

She let the curtains drop and turned back to look at Joe. He was sleeping deeply. God knew he could use it. Between his injury and their adrenaline-fed flight south to Nevada, he'd slept little in the past few days. She couldn't wake him now just to appease her curiosity.

But she couldn't just sit here and do nothing, either.

Moving silently, she shrugged on a light jacket, picked up one of the room keys from the bedside table and crossed to the door. As quietly as she could, she opened the door and slipped outside.

The setting sun brought dipping temperatures, carried on a light breeze that lifted her hair and made her burrow deeper into her jacket. She gazed up the busy street, feeling a bit disoriented, as if still trapped in whatever nightmare had jarred her awake. A vague sense of foreboding lingered with her, making her queasy.

She finger-combed her hair back from her face, trying to settle her still-rattled nerves. She felt the need to do something constructive with the last few hours of their time in Reno. But what?

To begin with, she could at least go down to the front office and buy one of the Reno city maps the desk clerk had told her about on the phone earlier. She and Joe had never picked one up, sidetracked by finding her father waiting for them outside their room.

The front office was little more than a small kiosk located at the western end of the squatty two-floor motel. A young woman about Jane's age, with short blond hair and pale blue eyes, looked up as Jane entered. Jane saw a flicker of recognition in the other woman's eyes and something clicked into place. "Ashlee."

The desk clerk's eyes widened. "So you remember."

Jane shook her head. "Not really. Just—pieces."

Ashlee flattened her hands on the glass top of the front desk, her expression guarded. "Long time no see."

"You're the one who told my father where to find me."

"I thought the old man would want to know."

"You still work for him?" Jane asked.

"No. Got out of that a few years back. I have a baby now." Ashlee reached for something under the desk and came back with a wallet. She opened it and showed Jane a photo of a little girl with blond ringlets and eyes as big and blue as her mother's. "That's Kathryn. She's two."

Jane smiled, although a phantom pain raced through her insides. She tamped it down. "She's beautiful."

"She's mommy's little angel." Ashlee put the wallet away and looked at Jane with a furrowed brow. "What happened to you, Shan? Why don't you remember anything?"

"I don't know," Jane admitted. "What do you remember about me?"

"We were friends—we kind of had to be, since we were the youngest in the crew. My daddy was your daddy's right-hand man. They planned a lot of the scams together."

"Did I tell you where I was going when I left Reno?"

Ashlee shook her head. "We'd drifted apart by then. My pop had gone out on his own, so we didn't see much of you and your pop anymore. I just heard you took up with some older guy and he took you out of here."

"Was his name Clint? Clint Holbrook?"

"I don't know. I never heard the name."

Another dead end, Jane thought.

"Are you and your fellow going to be in town long? Maybe my husband and I could take you out to dinner—"

Jane shook her head. "We're heading out of town soon. But it was nice to see you. Listen—on the phone this morning, you mentioned I could buy a city map here—"

Ashlee reached under the counter and pulled out a map. "Here. On me."

Jane took the map and smiled her thanks. "It was good to see you again, Ashlee."

"I hope you get your memory back, Shan. Some of the old times are worth remembering."

Jane smiled at Ashlee and gave a little wave before she headed out of the office into the waning sunlight.

"Going somewhere?" The sound of Joe's low drawl made her jump.

She whirled to face him, placing her hand over her pounding heart. "Don't do that!"

"What? Sneak around?"

She sighed and started walking back toward the motel room. "I just came down here to get that city map we never got earlier."

He fell into step. "Planning on a little sightseeing in the next couple of hours?"

"I thought we might go look for the Lady Luck if you woke up in time."

He put his hand on her arm, stopping her in the middle of the walkway. "You want to see your father?"

"I may never see him again," she said softly, surprised by the bleak emotion accompanying that thought. "I just don't want to leave without asking him a few more questions about my former life. Can you understand that?"

The hand on her arm moved gently, his touch becoming a caress. "Yeah. I can."

They returned to the motel room together and unfolded the map on Joe's bed. Jane found Pridemore Avenue on the map. "It's about twelve blocks from here."

"Better grab a jacket, then."

She looked at him. "We've got a long drive tonight once we get that rental car. I don't think you need to walk twelve blocks in the cold."

"You're not going by yourself."

"I know that. But I have an idea." She picked up the phone and rang the front desk.

Ashlee answered. "Front desk."

"Ashlee, it's Shannon Dugan," Jane said. "Do you have a car?"

PRIDEMORE is up ahead," Joe said from the passenger seat. He was playing navigator while Jane drove, though he'd questioned that arrangement when she admitted, as she belted herself behind the steering wheel, that she wasn't entirely sure she knew how to drive a stick shift.

But apparently she did, because she handled the borrowed Honda Prelude with skill, negotiating Reno's busy streets without any difficulty. He suspected that more of her memory was coming back to her—in pieces, perhaps, but sliding back into her consciousness little by little, making her feel more at ease with the world she lived in.

Joe could tell that she was growing nervous about seeing her father again. He laid his hand on her shoulder and gave a little squeeze. "It's going to be fine," he assured her. "We'll find Harlan, you can ask him the questions you want to ask him, and then we can go."

"I'm not sure what I want to ask him," she admitted.

"You said you think he knows more about Clint Holbrook than he's telling. You could start there."

Jane turned the Honda onto Pridemore Avenue and glanced his way. "How much farther?"

"Two blocks up, according to this map." Ashlee had given them the actual address of the Lady Luck, marking it for them on the map before she handed Jane the keys to the Honda. Joe wasn't completely at ease putting their safety in the hands of a former con artist Jane barely remembered, but having the car at their disposal would at least make them more mobile if they ran into trouble.

The Lady Luck Tavern was a two-story storefront building in the middle of the block, with only a neon beer sign in the window to differentiate it from the other shabby-looking shops and offices surrounding it. A small sign advertised parking in the rear, but Joe spotted an open parking slot on the street half a block up and suggested that Jane park there instead. "I don't want to get trapped in a back parking area," he explained.

Traffic on this part of Pridemore Avenue was light, and the cars parked along the street were older-model vehicles for the most part, a few of them well past their primes. As he and Jane crossed the street and headed for the tavern entrance, he noticed that the dark-tinted tavern windows allowed for no good look inside. It gave him an uneasy feeling, and on instinct he reached behind him to feel for the holster and weapon that wasn't there.

He dropped his hand back to his side and caught Jane's arm as she started for the door. "Wait a second."

She looked up at him. "What is it?"

Before he could answer, he heard a muffled cry coming from somewhere behind the building.

His instinct was to go back to the car and get the hell out of there, but Jane exclaimed, "That's my father!" and started running toward the narrow alley between the tavern and the insurance company office next door.

Cursing softly, he ran after her, grabbing her arm before she darted into the open area behind the building. "Wait a second!" he hissed.

The sounds of a struggle echoed through the alley, and Joe had to hold on to her to keep her where she was. "Someone's hurting him!" she whispered urgently.

"You stay right here." He crept forward to the edge of the building and peered around the corner.

In the dimly lit parking lot at the back of the bar, two large, muscular men took turns pummeling Harlan Dugan while the older man tried to fend off their blows.

It was a warning beating, Joe recognized immediately, not a real attempt on the old man's life. The thugs were pulling their punches too much to be really serious about it, like a couple of tomcats toying with a scared mouse.

He didn't see either man carrying any weapons, though he supposed they might have weapons concealed beneath their jackets or in their boots. It wasn't a risk he wanted to take, however. Not with Jane's life at stake, too. Better to call 911 and tell the cops there was an assault taking place in the parking lot of the Lady Luck. He turned to tell Jane his decision.

But she was nowhere in sight.

## Chapter Thirteen

Joe hurried up the alley, biting off a string of curses. He'd told her to stay put, damn it! Where the hell had she gone?

He had almost reached the street when two enormous men filled the narrow opening of the alleyway, carrying what appeared to be large nightsticks. They stopped short, apparently surprised to find him staring back at them.

*Bring it on,* Joe thought, his muscles tightening in anticipation of a fight.

Then Jane appeared around the edge of the building. "He's with me," she told them.

The two men nodded and moved past Joe toward the parking lot, where the sounds of a struggle still played out in muffled tones. Joe watched them go, not sure if he was relieved or disappointed.

"Bouncers," Jane said.

"So I gathered. I thought I said to stay put."

"I don't always do what I'm told." She tugged his arm. "We need to get back to the car."

He looked at her, surprised. "I thought you'd want to make sure your father is okay."

"Those two guys beating him up? Clint sent them." She started walking back toward the car at a fast clip.

"How do you know?" Joe asked, catching up with her.

"I asked around while the club manager went to get the bouncers. The girl who takes the cover charges said a couple of guys came looking for my father and said to tell him Clint sent them."

"He told Clint where we are. Damn it!"

"I know," she said, her jaw rigid as she turned to look at him. "He probably called Clint as soon as he left the motel." Her gaze shifted away from him, looking at something behind him.

Joe turned and saw Harlan Dugan emerge from the alley alone, staggering a little. Leaning against the wall, he lifted his head and looked in their direction. He lifted his hand in a small wave and turned away. Jane got behind the wheel without another word.

Joe rounded the car and slid into the passenger seat. "I'm sorry."

"I don't feel surprised, so I guess I'm used to it from him." She gripped the steering wheel so tightly her knuckles whitened. "I suppose he thought he was protecting me when he warned me to leave."

Joe looked back at the tavern. Dugan still slumped against the front wall, head down.

Self-serving son of a bitch.

"Good thing you suggested checking out of the motel before we left," Jane murmured.

"Yeah, no going back to the room now." He'd planned to take one last look around their room to make sure they hadn't left anything behind, but now they couldn't risk it. It would be risky enough to take the borrowed car back to the motel.

Joe didn't think Clint would connect Melissa Blake to him, at least not right away, even if he came to town and started checking all the hotel and motel registers in Reno. And she'd be flying back to Wyoming the next morning if everything went as planned.

Shortly before ten, they reached the motel where Melissa had booked a room. Jane cut the engine and turned to look at him. "Does your stepmother know I'm with you?"

He shook his head. "I couldn't risk telling her."

"Because she still thinks I killed her son?"

"Yeah."

Jane frowned. "So you're going to spring it on her when she gets here?"

"Well, I wasn't thinking of it quite that way—"

"What if she refuses to hand over the rental car?"

"We'll just convince her that you didn't kill Tommy."

Jane looked skeptical, but she settled quietly against the car seat, nibbling her lower lip.

Melissa's call came at precisely ten forty-five. "My flight got in a little early. I just picked up the rental car. Is everything still on?"

"Still on," Joe said, looking at Jane. "We're already at your motel, waiting for you."

Thirty minutes later, a silver Chevrolet pulled into the motel lot and parked a few slots down from where they waited. Joe saw his stepmother emerge from the driver's seat and look around. He got out and met her gaze across the tops of the cars parked between them. Melissa's dark eyes crinkled and she offered a hesitant smile.

Joe crossed to meet her, taking her overnight case from her. "Thanks for coming."

"You're welcome." A furrow creased her brow. "You look tired, Joe."

Joe blinked back hot tears burning his eyes and took her outstretched hand. "You look beautiful as ever."

She squeezed his hand. "I was surprised to hear from you. I suppose you must be really desperate."

He couldn't argue, though the flood of guilt pouring through him made him wish otherwise. "There are a lot of things I still don't understand about why you left without even keeping in touch, but those are questions that can wait until later." He led her to the borrowed Honda.

"I thought you brought me here to rent a car for you?"

"I did. This one's borrowed." He bent and looked at Jane through the driver's window. She rolled it down and met his gaze briefly before she turned her eyes toward Melissa.

"Sandra?" Melissa's voice went low and cold. Joe turned to find her gazing in horror at Jane. She turned on him, stiff with outrage. "What's she doing here? She killed my son!"

"I didn't kill him," Jane said softly.

Melissa wheeled around to face her. "Shut up, Sandra! You just shut up!"

"I go by Jane now." Jane lifted her chin and met Melissa's gaze.

"I don't care." Melissa turned back to Joe. "Don't let your emotions rule your head—"

"Like you did when you walked out on my father and me for your new boyfriend?" Joe shot back.

Melissa blanched. "That's not how it happened."

"We need to go if we're going." Jane shot Joe an apologetic look. "We're starting to cause a scene."

"You made the same mistake with Rita—"

He stared at her, surprised. "How do you know about Rita?"

"Canyon Creek isn't that big, Joe." Melissa looked at Jane, her expression dark and loathing. "Who are you hiding from?" she asked coldly. "The police?"

"Three days ago, someone tried to kill us. Twice," Joe said firmly. "He killed her roommate in Idaho. And I'm more and more sure he's the one who killed Tommy, as well. He knows we're in Reno. I'd rather he not find us."

"Mrs. Blake, I understand you have doubts about me," Jane said. "But Joe needs your help. Don't do it for me. Do it for him."

Melissa pressed her lips together, clearly struggling to control her emotions. She finally turned to look at Joe. "I said I would help you. I'll keep my word this time." She took her overnight bag from him and started walking toward the motel entrance.

Joe looked at Jane. "I'll be back in a minute. Lock the doors."

"She's going to call the cops the second we leave," Jane murmured.

"I'll talk to her some more."

Jane shook her head. "She thinks you've let your hormones control your head. Which reminds me—who's Rita?"

There wasn't enough time to answer that loaded a question. "Lock the door. I'll be right back." He hurried to catch up with his stepmother.

Melissa turned to look at him as he reached her side near the front desk. "You left her alone? How do you know she won't run?"

He took the bag from her again. "She could have run a half dozen times so far, and she didn't."

She looked up at him, her eyes troubled. "Before he died, Tommy told me you were in love with her. You still are, aren't you?"

Joe didn't know how to answer, so he just nodded toward the desk clerk waiting expectantly for them at the front desk. "Let's get you registered."

JOE SET his stepmother's overnight case on the bed and turned to her. "I owe you."

Melissa shook her head. "I owe *you.* I'll never forgive myself for walking away from you the way I did. You know that, don't you? You know how sorry I am?"

The old pain still lingered, tight and hot in the center of his chest. He shook his head. "We don't have time to get into who did what."

"I loved you. I never stopped. The day you found Tommy was one of the happiest days of my life. I always hoped you'd find a way to see him again."

"But you never told him about me. All those years, Melissa. You never told him."

Tears rimmed her eyes. "You and your father were a package deal. I knew that."

"So you hated my father so much that you were willing to walk out on a kid who thought of you as his mother and deny your other child his family?"

"*He* hated *me* that much, Joe. I couldn't live up to your mother's memory, and he never forgave me for that." She wiped her eyes with shaking hands. "I don't want to think about what all that hate would have done to Tommy."

"He never forgave me, either."

Melissa touched his hand. "You were her son."

"I was the reason she died."

She frowned. "You were a baby."

"I was a sick baby she drove to the hospital in a snowstorm the night she ran off the road and died."

Melissa stared at him. "He blamed you for that?"

Joe didn't answer, hating the way he felt inside, like the same vulnerable child who'd listened to his father's drunken tirade that cold December night twenty-five years ago—the first and last time his father had ever spoken to him about his mother's death.

"Bastard!" Melissa's voice shook with anger.

"I wanted you to come find me," he admitted. "I wanted you to take me to live with you and Tommy."

She reached out and brushed her fingers across his cheek. "I wish I had."

He fought his instinct to bury himself in her arms as he had so many times as a child, and he pulled away from her touch, regathering the steely control that had served him well for twenty-five years. "I have to go." He pulled out the roll of bills stashed in the front pocket of his jeans and handed her five hundred-dollar bills. "This should cover your expenses and the cab ride back to the airport."

She narrowed her eyes. "Where'd you get this?"

He smiled. "I'm very good at blackjack."

Melissa followed him to the door. "Be careful, okay?"

"I will. You do the same." He moved the Do Not Disturb sign around to the outside knob of her door. "Did you bring food like I suggested?"

"Yes."

"Good. That way you don't have to let room service or anyone else in. Just stay here overnight and leave as soon as you can in the morning, and you should be fine." He didn't think Clint Holbrook would connect Melissa to him—he'd had little to no contact with her in years—but he didn't like taking any more chances than necessary. "I'll be in touch as soon as I can."

He closed her door behind him and headed for the stairs, not willing to risk the elevator a second time. The fewer people who saw him, the better. Just in case.

Reno wasn't the sort of town that slept, and there were still people out and about as he crossed to where Jane sat waiting. She lowered the window and looked up at him with troubled eyes. "How did it go with your stepmother?"

"She won't call the police," he said, hoping he was right. "You ready to go?"

She nodded. "I'll go first. You follow."

"See you at the motel." He tapped the door and gave her what he hoped was a reassuring smile. But the closer they came to leaving Reno, the more he started to wonder if they were going to get out of town alive.

He checked his watch. Twelve-fifteen, he noted with growing unease. He'd lingered too long getting Melissa settled in her room. Clint Holbrook could be in Reno already. Maybe he'd already picked up their scent and was closing in.

Ahead of him, Jane pulled out of the motel parking lot and onto the service road. He started the Chevy and pulled out behind her, trying hard not to think of all the things that could have gone wrong with their plan.

JANE CHECKED her rearview mirror. Joe had gotten stopped by a traffic light a couple of blocks back, and though she'd considered pulling off the street to wait for him, she talked herself out of it. She was only a block from the Admiral Arms Motel. She drove on, pulling up next to the office and parking in the side lot where Ashlee had told her to park. She cut the engine and slouched low in the driver's seat, keeping an eye on her side mirror for signs of Joe's arrival.

She scooted lower in the seat as car lights swung toward her parking spot. When they passed, she let herself sit up until she could just peer over the dashboard.

A dark-colored sedan pulled up next to the office and parked in one of the three short-term parking slots at the front of the building. From where Jane sat, she could see only the back end of the car. The car shimmied a little— the driver getting out, Jane thought. She released her breath, chiding herself for being such a scaredy-cat. It was a motel. People checked in and out all the time.

She pulled her jacket more tightly around her, wishing Joe would hurry up and get there. How long could that traffic light have lasted?

Movement to her left caught her attention. Jane slouched lower again, trying to stay out of sight. At first, she could make out only two silhouettes. Both appeared to be male.

Then the taller man stepped into the glow of one of the floodlights positioned at either corner of the motel office, his features now discernible. Jane's heart skipped a beat.

It was Clint Holbrook.

## Chapter Fourteen

Jane peered over the back of the seat, doing her best to stay out of sight while she watched Clint Holbrook and a man who was clearly a motel employee climb the stairs to the second floor of the Admiral Arms Motel. Of course they were heading directly for the motel room that she and Joe had occupied until just a few hours ago.

They disappeared inside, and Jane turned around, releasing a quick sigh of relief as she reached for her cell phone. She punched a button and the display panel came up, complete with a "low battery" message. Holding her breath, she tried to call Joe's number.

The cell phone did nothing but beep a warning.

Punching the off button, she jammed the cell phone in her pocket and looked back at the motel. A light shone in the window of unit 214, so they were still inside.

Time to find a better place to hide while she could.

She scanned the parking lot for a hiding place that would still give her a decent view of Clint's car. There. The two metal trash bins at the far end of the lot would work. There was just enough space to squeeze between them, and the shadows would hide her from view without anything blocking her view of Clint's car.

She scrambled over the stick-shift console and slid out the passenger door as quickly as she could, pausing only to push the keys under the front passenger seat as Ashlee had asked her to do, and raced toward the trash bins. Within a few feet of them, the sickly sweet odor of rotting food assaulted her nose and made her eyes water, but she pushed on, sliding between the bins and ducking into the shadows. She could still see the back end of the sedan Clint had been driving.

She forced her frantic breathing to calm, pushing back a rising tide of anxiety, but it was no use. Panic had begun to set in, making her whole body shake. Any minute now, Joe would drive up in the rental car, unaware he was heading straight into a potential ambush.

And she had no way to warn him.

As Joe pulled up at the stoplight at the end of the block, he glanced up at the Admiral Arms Motel in time to see Clint Holbrook step up to the railing.

Adrenaline shot through him, taking his breath for a moment. He scanned the scene for any sign of Jane. He spotted the Honda parked in the employee lot by the office, but it was too dark to see if anyone was inside.

Did Jane even realize Clint Holbrook was there?

The light changed, and Joe drove past the motel, his heart racing. He kept his speed normal, careful not to slow down as he took a closer look at the Honda. If Jane was inside, she was down on the floorboard hiding, which suggested she might have spotted Clint.

If she was even still in the car.

He turned into the parking lot of a coffee shop about a block up the street from the motel and parked between a couple of SUVs. The lights inside the shop doubtless made mirrors of the plate-glass windows, making it easy to escape the notice of the scattering of patrons inside as he made his way toward the back of the parking lot, where a narrow alley stretched for a couple of blocks to allow access for waste-disposal trucks to empty the large trash bins behind the establishments.

He stuck to the shadows, moving stealthily up the alley toward the Admiral Arms Motel. He paused for a moment at the edge of the motel grounds, peering around the corner of the redwood fence separating the motel's parking lot from the narrow empty lot next door.

He spotted Clint Holbrook and a shorter man walking across the front parking lot toward the detached building housing the front office. They disappeared from sight around the front of that building.

Joe made a dash for the two tall trash bins sitting at the edge of the alley and started to squeeze between them when he realized he was not alone. Someone was already crouched low in the space. He skidded to a stop, cursing silently as his boots made a loud crunching sound on the loose gravel of the alley.

The crouched figure moved, launching herself forward. Joe caught a flash of red hair in a narrow beam of light shining between the bins.

"Jane!" he whispered.

The figure froze. "Joe?" she whispered.

"I'm right here."

She scooted backward toward him, unable to turn in the narrow space between the bins. He pulled her to him when she was in reach, wrapping his arms around her from behind and pressing his face into her hair. Despite the foul odors coming from the trash bins, she still smelled good, soap-and-water fresh with an underlying essence he would recognize anywhere.

"Clint's here," she whispered, rubbing her cheek against his.

"I know. I saw him."

She trembled wildly, her teeth making a faint rattling sound. He tightened his hold on her and peered through the narrow space between the bins. "Which car is his?"

"The black sedan parked closest to the edge of the building. That's its rear end there by the corner."

He pressed his lips to the back of her head and watched the black sedan for any sign of movement. A few long minutes later, the taillights lit up and the car began to back out of the parking lot. As the headlights swung toward the trash bins, Joe pulled Jane around, pressing his back against the tall metal trash container.

He waited a few seconds and peeked through the space again. He spotted the sedan turning left into light traffic. He waited until it disappeared from sight before he released Jane, turning her to face him.

"You all right?"

"I am now," she responded breathlessly before throwing herself into his arms.

He held her tightly for a moment before gently setting her away from him. "Let's go. I want to get to Twin Falls by daylight."

She frowned. "Twin Falls, Idaho? I thought we were heading to Wyoming."

"I don't want to take the most direct route, in case anybody's figured out where we're headed." He threaded his fingers through hers and led her down the alley toward the coffee shop where he'd left the Chevrolet.

"So, TELL ME about Rita," Jane said as they crossed into Wyoming just after sundown the next day.

Joe glanced at her briefly before returning his gaze to the highway. She'd been napping in the passenger seat since Pocatello, but he should have known he wouldn't make it back to Canyon Creek without the subject of Rita coming up again. She'd been too hyped about the close call with Clint Holbrook on the long overnight drive to Twin Falls, and by the time they found a dingy motel where they could rest a bit before continuing on to Wyoming, her adrenaline rush was long gone. She'd been asleep before she hit the covers of the sagging queen-size bed in their motel room.

"That bad?" she murmured, shifting in the passenger seat to look at him.

"Rita was—briefly—my wife."

"Oh."

He slanted another look at her, taking in her furrowed brow and narrowed eyes. "It didn't last a year. I really should have known it wouldn't, but a man in love—"

"So you were in love with her?"

"I wouldn't have married her if I weren't."

"Are you still in love with her?"

He hadn't expected that question. "I suppose once you love somebody, there's a part of you that always will. But Rita taught me a good lesson about love."

"What's that?"

He looked at her again. "Sometimes it's not enough."

She turned her gaze back toward the windshield, falling silent. The darkness hid the craggy hills they were traveling through, as well as the towering grandeur of the Grand Teton Mountains to the north. It was a shame; Jane had loved the mountains, thrived on the harsh demands of the wilderness. She'd have enjoyed seeing them again.

Unlike Rita, who'd scampered back East after the first big snowfall, Jane had helped his brother, Tommy, keep the ranch running through a rough Wyoming winter without complaint. It had been her grit that had convinced Joe that what he was coming to feel for her might last longer than a few short months.

"Rita was a photographer," he said aloud. "She freelanced. Fashion shoots, mostly. Some magazine pieces. She came to Canyon Creek on location for a big men's clothing designer who wanted a Wild West theme for his next line. She came to city hall with the production manager to check on permits for the shoot."

"And you were there?"

"I was there." His voice softened in memory. "She was beautiful. Like something out of a magazine herself. Long blond hair, eyes the color of the Wyoming sky, trying to dress like a native and not quite pulling it off…"

"Love at first sight?"

"Yeah." He sighed. "For her, too, or so she said."

"Did you follow her back East or did she stick around Wyoming?"

"She said she loved it here, and I'd already done my time away from Wyoming. She decided to stay, see if she could get some work in the Jackson Hole area. She had a good portfolio. Folks in Jackson Hole were happy to give her work. We got married a month after we met."

"That fast?"

He smiled at her surprise. "That fast. And you know, the first few months were wonderful. The first flush of love always is."

"What happened?"

"It snowed."

Jane looked at him. "What?"

"It snowed. Wyoming-style." He could laugh about it now, with some time and distance. "She was from New Jersey, spent several years living in New York City. I tried to warn her about the snow, but she laughed at me. She knew about snow, she said."

"But not Wyoming snow."

"She didn't understand how much there'd be. How it could limit life in a lot of ways for weeks at a time."

"So she left because of the snow?"

"Well, that and the rich guy she met up at one of the Jackson Hole resorts. He offered to take her back East and make her forget her rash decision to marry a cowboy cop, and she took him up on it."

"Bitch," Jane muttered.

Joe laughed again. She'd said the same thing the first time he'd told her the sad story of Joe and Rita, almost a year ago. "She's not. She just made a mistake. So did I. We were lucky to get out of it as easily as we did. We could have had kids to deal with."

Jane fell silent after that, her gaze turned back to the winding highway unfolding in the beams of the Chevrolet's headlights. A light wind had kicked up as night fell, and to the east, the lights of Jackson cast a faint gray glow on the low-slung rain clouds gathered over the horizon. By the time they crossed the Snake River, rain had begun to fall in fat, sporadic drops. If they were lucky, it wouldn't begin turning to snow before they reached their destination.

Jane broke the silence a couple of minutes later. "Were you in love with me?"

Joe tightened his grip on the steering wheel. He had figured this question would come sooner or later, once it became clear she was beginning to remember things about her life before Idaho. He'd just thought he'd have more time to think about it.

"I thought I was," he admitted.

Just before his brother's murder, he'd been thinking about asking her to marry him. It had been a big step, emotionally, to let himself think in terms of forever again. His first thirty-odd years hadn't exactly taught him to believe anything could last a lifetime.

But the woman he'd known as Sandra Dorsey had seemed to understand him. She'd appreciated his love of the land, had been patient with his emotional reserve. Time and again, she'd shown pluck and grit, two traits he admired. She'd been a good friend to Tommy and a tender, passionate lover to Joe. He'd wanted to believe that the secrets he saw in her eyes couldn't hurt them.

But they had.

"Did I love you?" she asked.

"You seemed to."

"But I'd told so many lies." Regret tinted her voice.

"Yeah. You had."

"I'm sorry."

"I know." Despite the dangerous circumstances—or perhaps because of them—being with her again had reminded him of everything that had attracted him to her the first time around. Her tough-mindedness. Her quick wit. Her kind heart.

"How far to Canyon Creek?" Jane asked.

"Another hour." The ranching town nestled in a grassy valley southeast of Grand Teton National Park. Almost everyone in the area raised some sort of livestock—horses, cattle, some sheep. Many of the working ranches surrounding the town had added guest-ranch facilities for tourists looking for the authentic cowboy experience.

"We're not going to your place, are we?"

"Not unless we want to get caught." He eyed the thickening clouds overhead. "We're going to see Canyon Creek's deputy chief of police."

"ARE YOU sure we can trust him?" Jane asked as she huddled close to Joe for warmth. The wind had picked up, swirling under Jane's collar and dotting her flesh with goose bumps, but luckily, the rain had held off so far, leaving them cold but dry on the walk to Riley Patterson's sprawling ranch house from where they'd hidden the rental car in the woods a half mile down the road.

"With our lives." Joe slid the key into the backdoor lock and let them into the kitchen. A lone light over the stove shed a soft gold glow over the neat, old-fashioned kitchen. A gas heater hissed softly in the corner, drawing Jane to it like a moth to flame. She warmed her hands in front of it, emitting a soft moan of relief.

Joe rested his hand on the back of her head for a moment, the touch gentle and affectionate. A rush of pleasure moved through her, warming her as surely as the heater. "Get out of that jacket. I'll see what Riley has in the way of food."

Over a dinner of microwaved soup, she asked him more about his friend. "You said you grew up together?"

"Our fathers were both members of the same cattlemen's association. We both worked on our family ranches and took part in cattle drives to the summer grazing lands together. When I decided to be a cop, Riley thought it sounded like a good idea, too." He chuckled. "His daddy never has forgiven me for that."

Jane finished her soup and took the bowl to the sink. Joe joined her there, drying while she washed. He put the two bowls on the dish rack by the sink, where they joined a couple of plates and three coffee mugs. His hand rested for a moment on one of the mugs, his brow furrowed.

Jane glanced at the clock on the microwave. Almost 8:00 p.m. "Isn't Riley working kind of late?"

"He likes working late. Keeps his mind off—"

"What?" she asked when he didn't continue.

"His wife Emily was a nurse—worked two twelve-hour shifts every weekend at a big hospital over in Casper. She didn't come back one weekend. The Natrona County Sheriff's Department found her car still parked in the hospital parking lot. A few weeks later, they found her body in a nearby lake."

"My God." Jane's forehead creased in sympathy.

"They never solved the case. Drove Riley crazy for a while, but he's back to himself now. Mostly." Joe folded the drying cloth and laid it on the counter by the sink.

He led her down a narrow hallway to a small room on the right. Joe turned on the light to reveal an iron-spindle bed covered with a colorful wedding-ring quilt.

"I feel like Goldilocks," Jane murmured.

He looked at her, his lips curving in a half smile. "You remember Goldilocks?"

"I think so. Little blond girl? Three bears? Porridge?" She chuckled when he nodded. "Amazing that I can remember fairy tales but I can't remember what brought me to Wyoming in the first place."

He motioned her toward the bed. She sat on the edge and looked up as he turned off the light, plunging the room into darkness relieved only by the faint glow of the kitchen light. He sat next to her on the bed, his weight shifting the mattress, making her slide up against him. He put his arm around her shoulders, keeping her close.

"I think we both know what brought you here."

She sighed, resting her head against his. "Clint."

"Clint," he agreed.

"Do you think he was telling the truth about being my husband?" she asked.

"I don't know. It doesn't matter. Marriages can be ended. I should know."

She reached up to thread her fingers through his where they lay on her shoulder. "At first I thought he was here to take me back with him, but now I'm not so sure."

"Why?"

"I was thinking about something he said that first day, when he was waiting for me in my apartment." She shivered, remembering the sight of Angie's bloody body sprawled across the kitchen floor.

Joe turned his face, brushing his lips against her temple. "What did he say?"

"He said, 'You have something I need.'"

"You didn't tell that to Hank Trent when he was questioning you. Why not?"

"I don't know," she admitted. "I don't know that it really registered with me until now."

"What could you have? I saw the police reports from when you first showed up in Idaho. They found you with nothing but the clothes on your back. No identification, only a few bucks in your pocket."

"What if—" She stopped short as Joe put his hand over her mouth. Then she heard it.

A door opening in another part of the house.

Joe pulled her quietly to her feet and led her into the hallway. They had gotten about halfway to the kitchen when they heard a male voice, answered by another.

Jane didn't recognize the first voice, but the second voice was as familiar as a recurring nightmare.

It was Clint Holbrook.

# Chapter Fifteen

Joe froze, pulling Jane to him, as he heard Clint Holbrook's voice in the kitchen. "You haven't even heard from your boss?"

"I told you about the call from Idaho," Riley Patterson answered. "If I hear from them again, you'll be the first person I contact."

Their voices seemed closer. Joe glanced across the hall at the closet door. What did Riley keep in there? Coats? Cleaning supplies? He couldn't remember, but he didn't have time to think it through. He eased the door open, breathing a sigh of relief to find the tiny space mostly empty except for a couple of suede work coats and a small table piled high with extra blankets.

It was a tight fit, but it would do. He pushed Jane into the cramped closet and pulled the door almost closed.

A sliver of light from down the hallway was all the illumination they had, but it was enough for Joe to see the terror in Jane's eyes. He stroked her hair, pressing his lips against her forehead to calm her, even though his own heart was galloping wildly. The scent of her filled the small space, spicy sweet and feminine. A shudder of pure masculine need ripped through him in response, but he tamped it down, his need to hear what Riley and Clint were saying taking precedence.

In the kitchen, Riley's voice had taken on a note of frustration. "I'm sorry the trail went cold in Nevada, but I'm telling you, Joe hasn't contacted me since he and the woman were in Boise a few days ago."

"Would you tell me if he had?" Clint asked coolly.

"Are you suggesting I can't be trusted?"

"Clint got to your friend," Jane whispered, her voice little more than breath against his throat.

Joe shook his head, though the first glimmer of doubt was nagging at the back of his mind. Riley hadn't been the same since Emily's death, had he? He'd been working late, eating poorly, losing contact with all his old friends—

"It's been a long day, Mr. Holbrook. I'd like to eat a little dinner and get some shut-eye. I'll be in touch." Riley's boot falls rang on the tile floor. A moment later, the back door creaked open. "Good night."

The door closed and for a moment there was only silence in the kitchen. Then Joe heard his friend mutter a string of curses he hadn't heard since Riley broke his collarbone in a football game their senior year.

Now was the time he should open the closet and go tell his friend he was there. But he didn't move, except to pull Jane's body closer to his, tightening his arms around her to ease her wild trembling.

If he were the only person at risk, he'd take the chance that there was a good explanation for Riley's involvement with Holbrook. But he wasn't going to risk Jane's life that way. They'd have to stay put, keep quiet and wait for Riley to settle down for the night. Then they could get out of here and figure out someone else who could help them work through the mess they were in.

He heard Riley's footsteps on the kitchen tiles, restless and heavy. Then the sound of water running in the kitchen sink, followed by the clink of glass against metal. Riley was probably getting a glass of water—

The bowls, he realized with a start.

"We left the bowls in the dish rack," Jane whispered.

Riley would notice. No matter how strangely he'd been acting over the past couple of years, he was still a good, observant cop. He'd know he hadn't left a couple of extra bowls drying on the dish rack. Or the damp drying cloth on the sink counter.

Maybe he'd think they'd come and gone. Their bags were still outside Riley's house, hidden behind a small clump of juniper bushes near the dilapidated storage shed behind the house.

He heard Riley's boot steps moving down the hallway, getting closer. He held his breath until Riley passed, his footsteps fading as he entered the bedroom. The creak of bedsprings and twin thumps of his boots hitting the floor caught Joe by surprise. Maybe Riley hadn't noticed the bowls in the dish rack after all.

Jane's fingers curled into the fabric at the back of his shirt, pulling it tight. A soft twinge of pain in his side came and went quickly, eclipsed by the pounding pulse of adrenaline flooding his body. He listened carefully for further sounds, but beyond another soft creak of bedsprings, he heard nothing for several minutes.

Carefully, he pushed the closet door open a few inches, praying Riley had oiled the hinges recently. It moved noiselessly, to his relief. He stepped out first, Jane following. He closed the closet door again, stopping it just before it latched.

A faint light from the kitchen still glowed—not unusual, given the depth of darkness out here in the sticks so far from the lights of town. He usually left a light glowing somewhere in the house himself, to keep from banging a shin or stubbing a toe in the dark.

He kept one arm around Jane as he looked back toward the two bedrooms. The door to Riley's room was open, but Joe couldn't see the bed from his vantage point in the hallway, and he didn't want to risk walking down the hall to check. He and Jane needed to get out of there now.

Walking on the balls of his feet to minimize the noise of his footsteps, he led Jane down the hall to the kitchen. They made it a few steps inside the warm room when the overhead light came on.

"Going somewhere?" Riley Patterson asked from behind them.

Joe whirled around, putting Jane safely behind him. Riley stood with his back flattened against the wall next to the refrigerator, his service weapon in his left hand and his right hand still on the light switch.

"I'm a careless housekeeper at best," Riley drawled, "but even I know when there are extra dishes stacked up by my sink, Joe." He looked behind Joe, his lips curving in a half smile. "Hey there, Sandy. Long time no see."

Jane stepped out from behind Joe, keeping her fingers tightly twined in his. "I go by Jane now."

Riley's half smile widened. "So I hear. Still with the amnesia?"

"Some things are coming back," she answered with a deliberate composure that almost hid the tremors Joe could still feel rippling through her body.

He tightened his grip on her hand. "We're going now, Riley. Nobody has to know we were here."

Riley's eyes narrowed. "Are you afraid of me?"

"Well, I might feel better if you put the gun down."

Riley looked down at the Glock still held at the ready in his left hand. He lowered it, tucking it into the back of his jeans. "Better?"

"Much," Jane answered before Joe could say anything. "I've had enough guns pointed at me for a lifetime."

Riley's expression softened a bit. "I reckon you have at that." He looked back at Joe. "I hear you got winged."

"It's nothing," he answered. "I heard you talking to a killer."

Riley's eyebrows notched upward. "A killer?"

"The man you were talking to here earlier. Clint Holbrook."

Riley frowned. "Agent Holbrook? You know him?"

"Agent Holbrook?" Joe asked.

"With the FBI," Riley said.

"He's lying to you," Joe said. "That man killed a woman in Trinity, Idaho. I saw him kill two Idaho deputies with my own eyes. He shot at Jane and me. He followed us to Reno, Nevada, and sent two bullies to beat up Jane's father. He's no more an FBI agent than—"

"Riley's right," Jane interrupted.

Joe turned to look at her. "What?"

She looked up at him, her expression troubled. "Clint really is an FBI agent," she said.

THE MEMORIES had come in a rush. The flash of the badge. The confident air. The knowing look he'd given her as he waited for her to acknowledge his presence.

It had been five days after her eighteenth birthday, and she had been waiting in line at the bus station in Reno, waiting to see how far the $372.00 in her pocket would get her.

He'd quietly come to stand by her, outside the line. She'd felt his interested gaze and finally turned to look at him, and that's when he'd showed her the badge.

"He said he'd had his eye on me for a while," she told Joe and Riley, her shaking hands tearing strips out of a paper napkin on the table in front of her.

"Why?" Riley asked, returning to the table with a couple cups of coffee. He set one in front of Joe and slid the other across the table to Jane.

"I'm not sure," she admitted. "It's just a piece of a memory. I don't know what happened next."

"Maybe he lied to you, too," Joe suggested.

"Joe, I checked him out as soon as he showed up a few days ago," Riley said. "He's who he says he is. The Denver field office confirmed he's a profiler who usually works out of headquarters in D.C. Denver claims Holbrook happened to be in Idaho on vacation when he heard about the murder in Trinity, and he called the Denver office to set things into motion to offer his services as a profiler."

"He played his own people, in other words," Joe said.

"That would be my guess," Riley agreed.

"Why did you hang up on me when I called from Boise?" Joe asked, his expression still a little wary as he looked at his old friend. Tension radiated from him, contagious. It made Jane's stomach hurt.

"Holbrook sent an agent from the Jackson Hole resident agency to babysit me until he could get here. The guy was walking in just as you called." Riley gave Joe a pointed look. "I was hoping you'd call me at home."

"I couldn't risk it." Joe glanced at Jane. She met his gaze, remembering their whirlwind tour of Boise as they tried to shake Clint and the Idaho authorities off their trail and make it to Reno unscathed.

"Why'd you come back, then?"

Joe turned his gaze back to Riley. "Because I needed help from people I trust. That's you, isn't it?"

Riley looked hurt. "God, Joe, how can you even ask that after all these years?"

"We've been shot at, framed and chased all over Reno," Joe responded, his voice tight. "Trust is a bit of a problem for me at the moment."

"You can trust me. I swear that on Emily's memory."

Joe's eyes grew bright with emotion. He reached out and clasped his friend's arm. "I know. I just needed to hear you say it."

"Whatever help you want, you've got it," Riley promised. "What do you have in mind?"

"Right now, I need a new base of operations. Somewhere nobody would think to find me." He glanced at Jane. "I think I might know the place."

Riley's eyes shifted from Joe's face to Jane's and back. A hint of a smile touched his mouth. "Old Curt's place up in the hills?"

Joe nodded. "Nobody would connect me to your great-grandfather's old hunting cabin. And you can't get there except by foot or horseback."

"Horseback?" Jane asked.

Both men looked at her.

"Do I know how to ride?" she asked.

BY NINE o'clock, Joe and Jane were heading into an icy rain as they wound their way up Sawyer's Rise. Riley had supplied them with oilskin ponchos for the ride, but the brisk wind drove rain into every available opening, leaving them both soaked before they were halfway up the mountain.

The borrowed Glock 9mm lay heavily in the holster tucked into the back of Joe's jeans. It was a strangely comforting feeling, having it there, even though Joe hadn't used his own service weapon more than once or twice in his career as a cop.

Livestock thieves he could usually handle without resorting to gunplay. Clint Holbrook was a different animal altogether.

Over the soft moan of the wind, Joe heard a rattling sound. He turned his flashlight toward Jane and saw her teeth chattering in the cold. She clung to the reins with white-knuckled fists, her thighs clamped tightly to Bella's sides as the chestnut mare picked her way up the rocky incline. Realizing the light was on her instead of the path ahead, she turned her head and squinted at him.

"Almost there," Joe called.

"Damned good thing," she said flatly.

He grinned and turned the flashlight back to the path, urging his own horse, Jazz, up the narrow trail with a murmured command and a squeeze of his knees against the gelding's sides.

Within a half hour, they reached the top of the rise, where Riley's great-grandfather Curtis Patterson had cut a small clearing to build his hunting cabin. It was a good bit more primitive than the cabin he and Jane had shared in Idaho, but it was shelter, with an electric generator, a water pump, a large fireplace and a wood-burning stove. A small horse shed behind the cabin would shelter the horses for the night in relative warmth.

"I'll settle the horses," he told Jane as they dismounted in front of the cabin's wooden porch. "The place is unlocked—nobody comes up here but Riley and me." He took the reins from her icy hands and nodded toward the cabin door. "Go on in and see if you can get a fire started. I'll be inside in a second."

He led the horses to the shelter and tied them in two of the shed's four stalls. Riley had been up there recently, he noticed with relief. There was fresh hay in the stalls and a large plastic barrel full of fresh horse feed. He gave each of the animals a rub down and made sure their beds were warm and dry before he gave them a little feed and some water, forcing himself not to skimp on attention to the horses just because he wanted to get back to the cabin where Jane was waiting.

Would she remember this place? Pieces of her lost memory were coming back to her, more and more every day. And the cabin was special to them.

Would Jane remember why?

JANE STRIPPED to her underwear and hung her clothes on the back of a chair in front of the cold fireplace. For the second time tonight she was soaking wet, but the quick shower at Riley's house had been a tropical vacation compared to the drenching she'd received on the ride up the mountain.

She was relieved to see someone had already left the makings of the next fire, with two fat logs and several kindling twigs already piled up, ready to use. Now she just had to find the matches.

Shivering, she wrapped a blanket around herself then searched the cabin until she spotted a small alcove that appeared to serve as a kitchenette. Scrabbling through the drawers, she found a box of matches and carried them back to the fireplace.

A strange sensation prickled the skin on the back of her neck as she opened the box of matches and withdrew one. This place seemed…familiar. In some ways, it was not so very different from the nicer cabin belonging to Angela Carlyle's family in Idaho. Rough plank floors, sturdy pine window frames, a stone fireplace instead of brick.

But the Carlyle place was just that. A place.

This cabin was a memory. Elusive, just out of reach.

She tried not to force it. That never worked. Instead, she struck the match she'd removed from the box and turned toward the fireplace.

The outside door opened, letting in a blast of cold, damp air along with Joe. He stopped in the doorway, staring at her for a moment. Then he shut the door behind him and walked toward her, his pace unhurried. His gaze moved over her body, as tangible as a touch.

Her heart rate tripled in the time it took for him to reach her. He took the match from her hand just as its heat began to reach her fingertips and tossed it into the fireplace. The kindling caught fire, shooting off sparks and light.

He moved away from her, stripping off his wet jacket.

Jane forced her gaze away from him, reaching for the hurricane lamp sitting on the mantel over the growing fire.

She found a wick trimmer sitting beside it on the mantel and set about lighting the lamp, wondering how and when she learned such a skill. Had it been here, in this cabin? Had Joe taught her?

She thought maybe he had.

She turned to look at him. Her breath caught. He stood closer than she thought, close enough to touch. Stripped to his damp jeans, his rain-slick body glistening in the warm glow of the fire, he seemed like a creature formed from the fabric of her deepest fantasies. Elemental, masculine and hers for the taking.

"I'll get the sheets for the beds," Joe said, his voice ragged.

"No, let me," she said, forcing her reluctant body toward the tall pine armoire standing at the foot of the closest bed. She had already opened it and taken out a set of sheets before she realized that she'd known exactly where to find the linens.

She turned back to the bed, afraid to let herself look at Joe, not yet ready for the trickle of memories to become an inundating flood that would wash her away. Clinging to her control like a shield, she returned to the bed slowly, stripping back the thin dustcover protecting the mattress, and started to make the bed.

She heard Joe's approach, slow steady footfalls across the plank floor. The heat of his body warmed the chilly air, the sensation bringing with it a steady stream of images racing through her mind. A crackling fire spreading light and warmth. Soft sheets beneath her back. Joe's body, hard and beautiful and relentless over her, driving her to the edge of madness and beyond. Her soft growls of release, echoed by his as they fought for every last ounce of pleasure.

Were those really memories? Or were they fantasies, her secret longings come to life in her imagination?

She finished making the bed and turned to face Joe, trembling. His eyes were wide and dark with an emotion that answered her questions.

"You're remembering," he said softly.

## Chapter Sixteen

Clint Holbrook unknotted his tie and settled back in his chair, looking around his shabby hotel room with disdain. If he never had to chase Sarah to another backwater hellhole again, it'd be too soon. What was her fascination with places like this? He'd shown her a life of ease, where she wore beautiful dresses and expensive jewelry and wanted for nothing.

Ungrateful bitch.

He might have been in love with her once, he supposed, the way a sculptor might obsess over his latest masterpiece. Until he saw that the flaws in the marble would never go away, no matter how he much he chipped and polished.

She was what she was. No changing that now. This time, he needed what she'd taken from him. And then he'd be done with her. For good.

His cell phone rang. It was Prescott from the Jackson Hole Resident Agency. "Got something for me?" Clint asked.

"I've e-mailed the passenger manifests you asked for."

Clint thanked Prescott and pulled out his PDA. He scanned the list of passengers flying between Jackson Hole and Reno over the last few days. One of the names caught his eye. It might be a coincidence, he thought. Not an uncommon name. But she'd flown to Reno the night before, and returned the next day. What kind of trip was that?

He made a note to find out where Melissa Blake lived. He'd give her a visit bright and early the next morning.

"YOU REMEMBERED where the sheets were kept." Joe's gray eyes glowed with a mixture of hope and fear. "You went right to the armoire. Tell me you remembered."

Tears spilling down her cheeks, she nodded. "I remember this place. I remember you." She flattened her hand against the center of his chest. His heart hammered wildly against her palm, matching beat for beat the pulse thundering in her ears. "I remember…this."

He threaded his fingers through her damp hair, lifting her face toward his. "Yes."

She put her other hand on his chest and smoothed her palms over his damp skin in slow circles, his hair rough beneath her fingertips. A strange certainty descended over her, easing the tremors rattling her nerves.

This was right. They were right.

She looked up at him through her tears. "We made love the first time right here. On the Fourth of July, after the big parade but before the fireworks."

He smiled, his thumbs moving over her cheeks, dashing away her tears. "We heard the booming from the cabin."

Laughter bubbled up in her throat as she pictured the scene so clearly, as if a cloudy glass wall standing between her and her memories had shattered, letting her see beyond. Though some pieces remained blurry, they couldn't hide the truth from her anymore.

Not about Joe. Not about who he'd been to her. Who she'd been to him.

She remembered lying with him, naked and spent, as the first fireworks blast had rattled the cabin walls. "You dared me to go naked to the bluff to watch the fireworks," she said aloud, slapping his chest lightly. "Cowboy Joe, who knew you had a naughty streak?"

He nuzzled her neck, his laughter tinged with wonder and relief, like a condemned man given a miraculous reprieve. "You certainly knew by the end of summer."

Fire scorched her nerve endings where he touched her. She arched her neck, giving him better access. "I'm still missing quite a few memories," she murmured.

He pulled back, which wasn't quite what she'd intended. "So you don't remember everything?"

The serious tone of his voice made her stomach knot. "Not everything. Does that matter?"

His brow furrowed with uncertainty, and she kicked herself for saying anything at all when he'd been doing such magical things to her throat with his lips and tongue.

Whatever she couldn't remember, whatever had happened to end the idyllic summer she was finally starting to remember, she didn't want it to destroy what was happening here between them.

"I remember enough," she murmured, sliding her hand up his chest. "I remember…I remember you feeding me chocolate in bed," she said.

The furrow in his brow disappeared.

"I remember that you can't carry a tune in a bucket."

His lips quirked. "I was told that serenading a woman was a very romantic thing to do."

She stroked his jawline. "Only if you can actually sing.

But I also remember that you're a whiz with birdcalls. You taught me a few, right?" She tried one, the shrill call of the American dipper. It was about the only one she'd ever been good at, despite its difficulty.

Joe laughed. "I forgot how good you are at that."

"I'm good at a lot of things." She curled one hand around his neck and pulled him down to her, parting her lips for his kiss.

He resisted for a moment, his body tense, but when she brushed her tongue against his, he surrendered, his hands sliding down her spine to settle on her hips. He backed her toward the bed, she hit the mattress and tumbled backward onto the cool sheets, bringing him down with her. She deepened the kiss, demanding more.

He gave it to her in hot, maddening kisses that trailed down her throat and over her collarbone to settle over the lacy cotton of her bra. He suckled one nipple briefly through the fabric before pulling the fabric aside with a frustrated groan.

He laved her hardened nipple, sending fire streaking through her body from that single ignition point. She threw her head back against the sheets, sensations tangling with memories. His mouth on her belly, tracing a slow, heated path downward. His fingers moving between her legs, seeking, exploring, teasing until she cried out for him to end the sweet torment. For a moment, she wasn't sure what was real and what was memory.

She felt his hand slide slowly over the curve of her hip. She caught it, pulling it between their bodies, urging his touch lower and lower. He drew back and gazed at her, a question in his eyes.

"Please," she whispered.

A wicked smile curving his lips, he moved his hand beneath the soft cotton of her panties and slipped his finger inside her, his touch bold, sure and achingly familiar. He knew her, even more than she knew herself at the moment. The intimacy of his touch was proof of that.

He knew how much she liked being touched that way, she remembered, her head swimming with images and sensations from the past. He knew when to tease and when to demand, playing her like an instrument until her whole body sang. He'd always found new ways to bring her to the edge with just his fingers and his soft, hot murmurs of encouragement.

He hadn't forgotten. She felt herself slowly coming apart beneath his touch.

"Is that good?" he whispered against her breast.

"Yes," she moaned as he found a sensitive spot. It had been a long time, and her body responded strongly, hurtling toward completion with coltish eagerness. Her back arched when he pressed the knot of nerves beneath his thumb. "Joe, please—not yet—"

He rolled away from her and stripped off his jeans. She started to reach for him, but he held back a moment, his brow furrowed. "I didn't really plan for this—but maybe we're lucky—" He leaned over and opened the drawer of the nightstand.

She propped herself up on her elbows. "The condoms are in the other nightstand," she murmured.

He looked at her over his shoulder, a slow grin spreading over his face. "The things you remember..."

She grinned as he stretched across the bed to the other nightstand and returned, triumphant, with a box. He shook it, and the foil packets inside rattled. "So far so good. Let's check the expiration date?"

"Should I hold my breath?" she asked, sliding her hand up the inside of his thigh. "Cross my fingers?"

He sucked in a deep breath as her fingers reached their goal. "Lucky for us, these are good for another year."

Darting her a look so full of naughty promise that her own breath caught, he pulled out a condom and ripped open the foil. With his other hand, he caught her roving fingers, stilling their movements. He turned her hand over and placed the condom in her palm. "Here. Since you're so eager to make yourself...useful."

Chuckling softly, she pushed herself up on her knees and straddled his lap, her tongue sliding over his as she sheathed him with the condom. "The things I remember," she murmured against his lips.

Then she lowered herself onto him, taking him deep.

Her whole body seemed to contract into one quivering, fiery nerve ending. She drew her head back and gazed into his eyes, her heart pounding so hard she was certain he could hear it.

"I remember you," she said, needing him to understand it was true. She didn't remember every detail of what they'd shared, or much of what had brought her to him in the first place, but she remembered how he'd made her feel. Safe. Special. Beautiful.

He brushed his thumb against her lips. "I see that," he said softly, pulling her down for another kiss.

Wrapping her arms around his neck, she rocked her hips forward until he filled her completely. His soft intake of breath filled her with a sense of power. Cradling his face between her hands, she made him look up at her so she could see the shift of his expression when she slowly withdrew.

"I missed you," he whispered.

Tears stung her eyes and she rocked forward again, lowering her mouth to his. She kissed him deeply, settling into a steady, escalating rhythm. Beneath her, his body grew taut with hunger. He was being patient, letting her set the pace, but she felt his muscles bunching as his need grew into something fierce and out of control.

*Now,* she thought, knowing what was about to happen more surely than she even knew her own name. She needed to feel him surge and take control, to remind her of his power as much as his patience had reminded her of his tenderness.

Memory intertwined with desire until she wasn't sure what was recollection and what was anticipation. She wasn't sure it mattered anymore.

Wrapping his arms tightly around her waist, he rolled her onto her back, pinning her beneath him. He threaded his fingers through hers, holding them above her head as he rose over her, gazing at her with hunger and a single-minded determination that thrilled her to her core. Dipping his mouth to hers to drink her kisses like a dying man, he drove into her, branding her with his desire.

As she clung to him, answering kiss for kiss, she began to unravel, swept into a maelstrom of pleasure that stole her breath and rocked her body. He plunged after her, his body shaking with release, urging her past sanity into a sweet madness as familiar as her own breath.

*She woke suddenly, as if startled awake by a noise, but the room was dark and silent. Only the faint metallic ticking of the clock on the fireplace mantel disturbed the quiet. For a moment, she wanted nothing more than to dive back* under the silk coverlet, as if it could protect her from the fear she lived with every second.

But she couldn't go back into hiding. She'd wasted the first few weeks back in Clint's control curled up like a scared child. That's not who she was. Not anymore. It was time to prove it.

She slipped on her house shoes and wrapped herself in the Chinese silk robe Clint had given her the first day back. He'd presented it as a gift, but she knew it was just a fancy sort of prison garb. She'd give anything to be back in her favorite fluffy green terry-cloth robe. Joe had teased her about it—"Sexy!" was his favorite comment when he caught her wrapped up in the thing—but he'd never let it stop him from stripping her out of it....

The thought of Joe made her smile all too briefly, before sorrow and longing overtook her. But she shook it off, pushed aside the memory of death and separation. Grief was weakness. She could no longer afford to be weak. She pressed her hand low against her belly, remembering why she had to keep fighting.

She tested the bedroom door. It was unlocked, though she'd half expected otherwise, given how easily Clint seemed to read her thoughts since he'd brought her back with him. Still, she knew the outer doors would be guarded, and the gates beyond locked and unbreachable. It had taken her almost two months to figure out a way to escape the fortress Clint had built to keep her with him this time.

Now she just had to decide when to make her move.

It had to be soon. Clint was beginning to notice that she'd stopped cowering, even if he didn't yet know what was driving her to fight this time around. But within a *month or two, he'd know exactly what was fueling her need to get away. She had to get out of here before that happened.*

Every night for the past few nights, she'd tested the limits of her prison. Tonight, Miguel had promised he'd leave the code for the back gate in the plant by the kitchen window. She'd retrieve it tonight, memorize the code and destroy the paper it was written on.

As soon as she found a chance, she'd escape the house and grounds. Then she'd get word to Joe somehow.

He'd come for her if she needed him.

In the corridor outside her bedroom, dim wall lights lit the path to the stairs. She padded quietly down the curving stairway to the first floor, where she heard the faint murmur of voices. She looked around for any of the house staff, but they'd apparently retired for the night. Taking a deep breath, she moved silently toward the room at the end of the hallway, where a door was barely cracked open.

She peered through the narrow opening and saw the back of Clint's head. He sat in a large leather chair, looking at the screen of a notebook computer. On the screen, a video was playing—the source of the voices she'd heard.

The picture was grainy but she could discern enough of what she was seeing to recognize Tommy Blake's horse barn. Her heart clenched at the sight of her friend walking into the picture, a feed bucket in one hand and a couple of blankets tossed over his shoulder. This must be from the surveillance system Joe had helped his brother set up in the horse barns to deter the rustlers who'd been creating havoc in the area that summer.

*Behind Tommy, Clint stepped into view. Tommy must have heard something, for he turned to face the other man, his expression wary but not yet afraid.*

*"Can I help you?" Tommy said.*

*Without saying a word, Clint took out a gun and pulled the trigger. Tommy's body jerked and he flew backward onto the hay-strewn floor of the barn.*

*She pressed her hand over her mouth to keep from crying out. Clint must not have heard her behind him, because he punched a button and the picture reset to that same moment when Tommy walked into the barn, oblivious to the fact that he would be dead in just a few more seconds.*

*With escalating horror, she watched Clint replay the murder again and again on the computer screen. Part of her wanted to run back to her bedroom and hide again, but another, stronger part of her realized that for the first time since Clint Holbrook walked into her life, she had proof that he was the bastard she knew him to be. She just had to find out where he kept the recording of the murder, get it to Joe and she'd finally be free.*

Jane woke in a rush, panic icing her veins until she realized she wasn't back in that bedroom prison but lying curled up in Joe's strong arms. The dream she'd awakened from was already starting to drift into the ether, but she struggled to hang on to it, forced herself to separate the misty threads of dream from memory.

Was it real? Had she seen a video of Tommy's murder?

She eased herself out of Joe's arms, soothing him with a whisper when he stirred, and slipped from beneath the covers. Frigid air washed over her naked body, making her gasp. She grabbed a thick thermal blanket from the armoire to wrap around her and crossed the hard plank floor to the cabin's front window.

Outside, the first faint gray of sunrise peeked over the top of the pines and aspens between the cabin and the bluff beyond. Beyond the bluff, where Tommy's ranch sprawled across 250 acres of grazing land, sunrise came a little later in the morning, having to rise over the ridge to the east before spilling light over the valley.

She remembered. She remembered everything now, the last clouds breaking in her mind to reveal her hidden past. She remembered who Shannon Dugan was, the hardscrabble life she'd lived. The cons, the scrapes with the law. She remembered who Sarah Holbrook was, too. Not Clint's wife—he'd never have sullied his family name by bringing her into it—but he'd treated her as his woman, taken her out of Reno and made her his lover, his pupil and, eventually, his partner in crime.

She'd been eighteen and foolishly in love. Too foolish to realize that the designer dresses, the etiquette lessons and the free access to his library weren't a reward for being his woman, but a means to an end. She'd become his shill in the political power plays that had given him more power than even his father's billions could do. He'd told her it was part of his job, that she was helping him do good deeds, but she'd grown up on the streets of Reno. She should have known better.

She just wanted to believe that kind of life was over.

She heard Joe stir behind her and turned, looking at him in the dying glow of the fire. He rolled to her side of the bed, throwing his arm over her pillow, and settled back to sleep, his face soft and boyish in slumber.

She had been so happy last night, lying in Joe's arms,

listening to the sound of his heartbeat under her ear. She had thought there was nothing that could separate them again. Not Clint, not the still-missing pieces of her past. But that was before she'd remembered the rest of it.

She crossed quietly to the bed and crouched beside him, tears burning her eyes. There was so much he didn't know about her because she hadn't wanted him to know what a fool she'd been.

It had cost them everything. And now that she knew the truth, she wasn't sure if they'd ever be able to get back any of what they'd lost.

But if it was possible, she now knew where to start.

She found her clothes and dressed quickly, taking care not to wake Joe. Shrugging on her fleece-lined jacket, she started out the cabin door, pausing a moment in the open doorway to look back at Joe. He hadn't stirred.

Dashing away her tears, she slipped out of the cabin and headed for the horse shed.

THE SUN was high when Joe finally woke. He wiped his gritty eyes and turned over, automatically reaching for Jane. But she wasn't there.

He pushed himself into a sitting position, looking at his watch. It was after nine.

"Jane?" he called, looking toward the tiny bathroom off the main room. But there was no answer.

He found his jeans on the floor and pulled them on. "Jane?"

A quick look around the cabin assured him she wasn't there. He finished dressing and went outside.

"Jane, are you out here?" Joe descended the cabin's wooden steps and landed on the damp grass. From the horse shed around the side of the cabin, Jazz's soft nicker answered him. Had Jane gone to see about the horses when he overslept?

He entered the horse shed and stopped, staring at the empty stall next to Jazz's. Bella's saddle and reins were also missing.

*Oh, Jane,* he thought, his heart dropping like lead. *What've you done?*

SHE WAS lost.

She'd thought the return of her memories would make it easy to find her way back to town, but last night's rain had washed out some of the path, and she was now certain she had been traveling in circles since daylight.

Jane wiped her sweaty brow with the back of her hand and checked her watch. Almost ten o'clock. She'd been out here for over three hours and was no closer to finding the horse trail than she had been when she left the cabin.

Blinking back hot tears of frustration, she pulled her horse to a stop and dismounted, stretching her aching legs. What the hell was she doing? Why had she run away, yet again, from the one man she'd ever known who seemed to care about her for who she was, not for what she could do for him? Why couldn't she just trust him as he'd asked her to do so many times?

*Because he didn't trust you the one time it really counted,* a small voice whispered in her ear. When she'd gotten away from Clint the last time, when she'd fought her way back to Joe despite one disaster after another, she'd learned just how little faith he had in her.

*The entire east wall of his living room was a giant bulletin board, packed from corner to corner with notes, newspaper clippings, enlarged photos of her time in Canyon Creek and faxes from dozens of Western law-enforcement agencies with reports of possible sightings.*

*He wasn't trying to save her from Clint,* she realized with dawning horror.

*He was trying to arrest her for Tommy's murder.*

He'd been out of town when she'd arrived in Canyon Creek a couple of weeks after she'd escaped Clint the last time. Weak, brokenhearted and desperate for a friendly face, she'd let herself into his house, hoping to find some clue to where he'd gone.

What she'd found was his shrine to his brother's murder and the woman he believed responsible.

What happened next was mostly a blur. She remembered a knock on the door. A quick glimpse out the window and the nightmare of seeing Clint Holbrook standing on Joe's front porch. The frantic scramble to hide the one piece of evidence that would prove her innocence, though too late to salvage her fragile relationship with Joe. Then she'd fled out the back door, never looking back.

It was the last thing she remembered before Idaho.

She patted the side of her horse. The mare snuffled softly in response, nuzzling Jane's jacket pocket, where she'd stashed a small bag of feed in case she needed it. She wished she'd brought a bottle of water as well, but she hadn't wanted to go back to the cabin and risk waking Joe. Stupid mistake. She should have taken a chance on him. Trusted him enough to tell him what she remembered.

Maybe it would be easier finding her way back to the cabin than trying to find the trail off the mountain.

She heard the soft snort of a horse moving up the rise

toward her, carrying through the cool morning air. Joe, she thought, her pulse quickening.

She grabbed Bella's reins and tugged her forward, so relieved to hear the sound of another living being that it never occurred to her, until the rider and horse rounded the bend, that her rescuer might not be Joe Garrison.

# Chapter Seventeen

The muzzle of the sleek black pistol twitched toward Jane. "Let go of the horse."

Jane stared up at Clint Holbrook, fear and anger battling for control. Anger won, but she knew she'd have to play scared awhile longer. Let him think he'd won.

She released Bella's reins. The mare looked at her as if waiting for direction.

Clint drew his mount up beside the mare and slapped the chestnut on the rump with his reins. Bella jerked and cantered a few steps away, then stopped to gaze back at them, clearly confused.

Clint ignored the mare and gestured for Jane to give him her hand. He reached his left hand toward her, the pistol still aimed right at her forehead, forcing her to give him her hand and allow him to haul her up on the horse in front of him.

The saddle horn made for a tight fit, forcing Jane to settle snugly between Clint's thighs. She gritted her teeth against a wave of nausea, reminding herself that she could bear anything for the chance to make Clint pay for what he'd done to her and the people she loved.

"What do you want from me?" she asked, even though she knew the answer. But she thought it might be safe for Clint to believe she still had amnesia. "Who am I to you that you've chased me across three states and killed an innocent woman and two deputies just to get your hands on me?"

Clint laughed. "You're a fugitive, darling. Don't you remember? Wanted for extortion in Maryland."

A lie, of course. He'd held that charge over her head for years, threatening to let the feds know how she'd stolen personal items from several influential congressmen and used them to extort information from the politicians. Information Clint had used to position himself to call in favors that had not only enriched his already massive bank account but given him the means to make further inroads into the personal lives of other powerful lawmakers.

But she realized now that she could easily turn state's evidence and make Clint's life a living hell. She wasn't alone anymore, without anyone to watch her back.

She had Joe.

Despite the gun pressed into her rib cage, Jane had never felt quite so free in her life. Joe would help her. No matter what lies she'd told him, no matter what doubts he might still harbor about her, as soon as he woke to discover her missing, he'd be on his horse to find her.

Clint reached around her. He had a small, sturdy hank of white rope in his left hand. He nudged her side with the gun. "Put your hands on the saddle horn."

She did as he said, acutely aware of the gun muzzle in her side. Clint wrapped the rope around her hands and the saddle horn, fastening her in place. He sat back when he finished. "You took something from me, darling. When we were living in Colorado. Do you remember any of that?"

She hid a smile. Clint must have been terrified to discover the DVD of Tommy's murder had gone missing from the safe where she'd seen him hide it. Cracking the safe had been a cinch; there were a few skills Harlan Dugan had taught her that she'd never told Clint about.

"I told you I can't remember."

"You obviously remembered your father."

"Yes. But that's all."

"What about the cowboy? Do you remember him?"

"Not from before," she lied.

"But you know you were his whore, right?"

She clenched her jaw. "Like I was yours?"

"Exactly," he growled, his grip tightening around her waist. "But I paid better. You'd do well to remember that, sweetheart."

He fell silent as they reached a steep drop in the path. Jane fought the urge to look behind them for any sign of Joe to the rescue. The last thing she wanted was for Clint to raise his guard. What she needed was for Clint to make a mistake. And soon.

JOE CAME across the chestnut mare, her reins tangled in the low-hanging limb of a cottonwood tree, about a quarter mile west of the cabin, but there was no sign of Jane. Tamping down the swift rush of alarm, Joe dismounted and tied Jazz's reins to another branch, taking a quick look around in case Jane had taken a fall. Up ahead, where the side path merged with the main bridle path, he found fresh horse tracks in the dirt—one set moving up the mountain, followed by a slightly fresher set moving away.

He left the mare tied to the cottonwood and mounted Jazz, pushing him into a somewhat reckless canter. The trail could be treacherous at any rate of speed, but the gelding was sure-footed, and Joe was a seasoned rider. He could tell from the tracks he was following that whoever he was following wasn't moving fast, probably because the horse was now carrying two riders rather than one.

He rode hard for another quarter mile before he caught sight of movement in the trees ahead. Pulling up, he peered through the wall of pines and aspens. There. A flash of gold, a flicker of white—a palomino bearing two riders, he ascertained after a few more seconds. They were about seventy yards ahead, in a place where the bridle path took a wide, curving detour around a rocky outcropping.

Joe dismounted, tying Jazz's reins around a nearby sapling, and continued on foot, staying close to the boulders, using them for cover. Because he could move straight ahead on foot, while the riders were forced to stick to the bridle trail's elliptical detour, he ended up ahead of them on the trail, where he waited, gun in hand, for them to ride into view.

He crouched low, hidden behind a large boulder and screened by the scrubby remains of a fallen lodgepole pine sapling. Through its needles, he spotted the riders as they passed a large cottonwood and came into view.

Jane rode up front, while Clint Holbrook sat behind her. His left arm held the reins, while his right hand seemed to be pressing against Jane's right side. Was he holding a gun to her side? Holbrook's face was half-hidden by Jane's head, but Joe had a full view of Jane's grim expression. As they drew closer, he saw the ropes binding her to the saddle horn.

He couldn't make a move, not if Clint was holding a gun to her side. But he couldn't let them get much farther, either. He knew this mountain like the back of his hand, but there were only a few shortcuts to help him keep pace. He couldn't keep up on foot for long.

He needed a distraction. And that would require Jane's help. He just had to figure out how to let her know he was there without tipping Clint off to his presence.

THE PALOMINO was tiring, and so was Jane. Riding up the mountain the night before had been her first horse ride in over a year, which would have been enough to make her muscles sore even before she spent the next few hours making love to Joe. Between her aching legs, the uncomfortable cramped position she was in and the rope burns on her wrists, she'd reached the end of her tether.

Where the hell was Joe?

A prickly feeling tightened her stomach. He should be up by now. He should know she was missing. But they'd been riding for nearly an hour now and she'd seen no sign of Joe during the handful of times the trail wound around itself, giving her the chance to peek sideways toward where they'd just been.

A new, paralyzing thought seized her, almost toppling her from the saddle as her whole body went numb. What if Clint had gotten to Joe first, before he met up with her on the trail? She'd been riding around, lost, for a couple of hours before she ran into her captor. He could have been to the cabin, done away with Joe, and circled back to find her just off the trail.

No. Her mind shut down at the thought. She gripped the saddle horn more tightly, closed her eyes and forced down the nausea knocking at her throat. She concentrated on listening to the sounds around her, grounding herself in the tangible rather than dwelling any longer on worst-case scenarios. She heard the clatter of the palomino's hooves on the rocky trail, the whisper of wind in the pines overhead. The shrill cry of an American dipper sounded from the underbrush a little behind them, reminding her of Joe's birdcall lessons.

They'd just talked about that last night. She'd done the call for him to distract him from the unknowns that had remained after her first flood of memories....

The cry came again, and Jane suddenly remembered something else Joe had told her about the American dipper. It was a water bird. But there were no streams, lakes or ponds anywhere on Sawyer's Rise. Her spine straightened. Her heart rate doubled with excitement.

It had to be Joe.

She tugged surreptitiously at her bindings. She'd been loosening the ropes as they rode, working slowly to keep Clint from figuring out what she was doing. With one little pull, the ropes slipped off the saddle horn. She wrapped her hands around the horn again, hoping Clint wouldn't notice that the ropes were no longer around it.

Now she had to figure out when to make her move. Right now they were on rocky ground, moving downhill again. A fall here could be disastrous. But about a hundred yards ahead, the trail flattened out again, with grassy shoulders along either side of the path.

That's where it would have to happen.

She bided her time, taking care not to tense up or do anything to draw Clint's attention. She had to catch him by surprise, and she thought she knew exactly how to do it.

They reached the flat stretch, and Jane took a couple of slow, steadying breaths. Then she sprang, jerking her hands free as she gave the palomino a hard kick in the ribs, trying not to feel guilty about harming the animal.

The horse bucked and reared, giving Jane the needed distraction. She flung herself off the horse, hitting the grassy shoulder with a painful thud. The air whooshed from her lungs, and dark spots swam in her vision.

Please help me, Joe, she thought, gasping for breath.

FROM HIS hiding place behind a scrubby pine sapling, Joe watched Jane hit the ground hard, and for a second, his heart stopped. Then he saw Holbrook bring the palomino under control, swing out of the saddle and move toward Jane, his weapon leveled.

Aiming the borrowed Glock at the FBI agent's mid-section, Joe walked out into the open. "Drop it, Holbrook."

Clint looked at Joe in surprise, but his aim never wavered from Jane. A feral smile split his face. "Well, if it isn't the cowboy riding to the rescue. We've got ourselves—what is it you bronco busters call it? A Mexican stand-off?" He looked back at Jane, who had finally caught her breath and lay in a half-fetal position, sucking in air in deep draughts. "Can you shoot me before I shoot her?"

"Shoot him," Jane growled breathlessly, gazing up at Joe from beneath the tangle of red hair that had tumbled over her forehead.

A soft rattle of rocks drew Joe's gaze briefly to the side. Riley Patterson emerged from behind a stand of lodgepole pines, a rifle aimed at Clint Holbrook's head. "The real question, Agent Holbrook, is which one of us gets to shoot you first."

Holbrook turned to look at Riley, his aim drifting to the right of Jane. She scrambled up and raced toward Joe, blocking his aim at Holbrook, but it didn't matter. Three more Canyon Creek police officers appeared on the bridle trail from their hiding places in the pines, weapons pointed at Holbrook.

Holbrook slowly laid his pistol on the ground and raised his hands. "Patterson, you're making a big mistake here. They're the fugitives. I'm trying to stop them."

"Cuff him," Riley told the other officers.

WHILE THE officers moved toward Clint to take him into custody, Jane flung herself at Joe, wrapping her arms around his waist and burying her face in his chest. He tucked his gun in the back of his jeans and whirled her around, putting himself between her and the others.

"How'd Riley know to come here?" she murmured against his neck.

"There's a cell tower in the valley just past the bluff. They added it last year. I gave Riley a call before I came out to look for you." He grinned at her, relief shining in his eyes. "Ain't technology grand?"

"I love you," she said, reaching up to hold his face between her hands. "Do you hear me? No matter what else you hear about me in the next few hours, know that I love you." She hugged him again, looking over his shoulder toward the knot of police officers surrounding Clint.

Suddenly, Clint looked right at her, his blue eyes cold and hard. A mean smile creased his face. And he turned toward the officers who were pulling his hands behind his back to apply the cuffs.

Clint's right hand found the holster of one of the officers, withdrawing the gun tucked inside. He broke free of them, pushing one policeman into the other two, knocking them all to the ground. Rushing past Riley, who turned too late to stop him, Clint raised the stolen gun toward Joe's back and met Jane's gaze over Joe's shoulder.

Jane reached behind Joe's back and jerked the pistol out of his waistband. She had no time to think, just pulled it up and pressed the trigger. Once. Twice.

Clint's gaze widened with surprise. The hand holding the gun fell to his side, the pistol thudding to the ground. He fell to his knees, toppled face forward into the grass, and went deathly still.

Joe let go of Jane and whirled around. Jane saw his body grow stiff with horror as he spotted Clint's body on the ground and the stolen gun just beyond his outstretched arm.

Riley crossed to Clint, kicking the gun away from his still form. He crouched and felt for a pulse. Looking up at Joe, he shook his head.

Jane pressed her face to Joe's back and started to cry.

"ARE YOU sure you're up for this, Joe?" Riley asked as they entered Joe's house near the edge of town a couple of hours later.

Joe looked at Jane, whose red-rimmed eyes gazed back at him with a mixture of love and anxiety. He caught her hand and squeezed. "Let's see it."

Jane released his hand and crossed the room, pausing a moment to look at the makeshift bulletin board where the remains of his investigation still hung from tacks and tape across the entire east wall.

He walked over to her, placing his hands on her shoulders. He pressed a kiss to the back of her head, knowing words weren't sufficient.

She squared her shoulders beneath his hands and moved past the clippings to the upright piano situated in the corner. She ran her hand over the dusty key guard, wiping her hand on her jeans, a half smile curving her lips, and he knew she was remembering the times she'd played the piano for him when they were together. Then she lowered the panel in front, revealing the hammers and strings, along with a small DVD case tucked between the last two strings on the right. She handed it to Joe.

"Now you'll know exactly what happened to Tommy."

"Why do you think he kept this?" he asked. "Did he tell you?"

Jane shook her head. "I think he liked to watch it." Her voice came out low and strangled. "Relive it over and over."

"Sick bastard," Joe murmured.

"I'm so sorry, Joe."

He touched her face, brushing away the tears under her right eye with his thumb. Then he took the disc to the DVD player across the room and pressed Play, steeling himself to see the answers he'd sought for over a year.

IT WAS almost nightfall before the FBI finished debriefing them and Riley told them they were free to go. The FBI agents assured them they believed their story about the murder of the deputies in Idaho, and that there would be no charges pending under the circumstances.

Joe had driven Jane back to his house and was now in the kitchen, brewing coffee and heating some chicken soup in the microwave, while she curled up on the sofa and reacquainted herself with a part of her past she'd once feared lost to her forever.

Joe came into the room bearing a tray with steaming

cups of coffee and two bowls of soup. He laid the tray on the coffee table and sat next to her. "Warm yet?"

She nodded, taking the mug of coffee. She breathed in the dark aroma, steeling herself for the final part of the story that she hadn't yet told Joe.

"There's one more thing I have to tell you," she said.

He took the cup from her hands and set it aside, threading his fingers through hers. He kissed her knuckles. "I love you. I fell in love with you about two minutes after I met you, and not one moment of the hell we've been through since then was able to change that. There's nothing you can say now that will change anything."

She smiled at his words, so sincere and heartfelt. She knew what it had cost him to let himself love her the first time—what it had cost him to take that chance again, in the face of her lies and secrets. But her last secret belonged to him, too, even if he didn't know it.

"When I left here, I was pregnant," she said, blurting it without preamble because there was no good way to prepare him for the truth.

He sat back, a half dozen different expressions fluttering over his face—surprise, confusion and, most heartbreaking of all, a flicker of hope. "We had a baby?"

She tightened her fingers around his. "I lost the baby, Joe. Right after I got away from Clint."

"Oh, honey." He stroked her cheek, brushing away a tear she hadn't even realized she'd shed. "I'm so sorry you went through that alone. Why didn't you call me?"

She licked her lips, wondering if she should spare him the rest of the story. But she didn't want any more lies, any more secrets, standing between them. "I came here. To find you. I needed to find you."

She made herself tell him everything—how she'd escaped from Clint's compound only to start having contractions immediately, how she'd lost the baby at a nearby hospital, then fled soon after being checked out when she heard Clint arrive, demanding to see her. She'd barely gotten away.

"Then I made my way here," she said, wiping the tears from her eyes.

"And saw that wall," he said, as if realizing for the first time what it must have been like for her to see the clippings on the wall, evidence of his loss of faith in her. He stared at her a moment, his eyes wet and his face twisted with regret. Then he lurched from the sofa and threw himself at the wall of clippings, ripping away the pictures and articles he'd tacked there.

She ran to his side, pulling his hands away from the wall. He resisted, his eyes dull with pain. "Stop it, Joe."

He dropped his hands to his sides, lowering his head until his chin nearly rested on his chest. "I'm so sorry, Jane. I shouldn't... I didn't really think you'd... But I was angry and hurt..."

She took his hands in hers. "We both made mistakes. I should have trusted you with the whole truth in the first place, and maybe Tommy would still be alive."

He met her gaze with pain-dark eyes. "Did he ever tell you why? Why he killed Tommy?"

She licked her lips. "He didn't want any witnesses when he took me out of here. It was all part of the power trip he was on. Nobody took anything that belonged to him. And he thought I belonged to him." She looked away.

"Scary to think he was in the FBI all those years and nobody suspected anything," Joe said.

"He hid it well. I think maybe that's what attracted him

to that job in the first place," she said softly. "All that power…" She looked up at Joe. "If only I'd been braver. I could have told someone what I knew and then maybe Tommy—"

He shook his head, cutting her off. "No, damn it. We're not going to do this to ourselves. It wasn't your fault. It was Clint's. Don't take any of the blame away from him."

"You're right," she agreed. "Clint's the one to blame."

He touched her hand. "What happened after you came here and hid the DVD?"

"I don't remember. There are two weeks missing between then and when I showed up in Trinity, Idaho. It's possible I'll never remember what happened during that time."

"Oh, baby…"

She took his hand and squeezed it. "It's over now, isn't it? We're still here. I still love you. You still love me, right? We made it."

He caught her face between his hands, the intensity of his gaze making her breath catch. "I do love you. I never stopped, no matter how hard I tried to make it go away." He pressed his forehead to hers.

"I know," she said softly.

He made a soft, sobbing sound and then crushed her to him, slanting his mouth over hers.

She kissed him back fiercely, giving him her strength and love in equal measures. He edged her back toward the sofa, drawing her down into his lap as he deepened the kiss. A few moments later, they broke apart, breathing hard, and gazed at each other in the ensuing silence.

"You're marrying me," he said. It wasn't a question.

"Damn straight," she said, wrapping her arms around his neck.

He lifted her into his arms and carried her into the bedroom. She tugged at the buttons of his shirt, needing to feel his skin beneath her fingers, to hear the pounding of his heart beneath her ear, beating out a cadence of hope and reassurance.

They were alive.

They were together.

As night fell, they reclaimed a life almost lost to them, washing away their lingering pains and fears in a flood of passion, pleasure and love.

"What should I call you?" Joe asked much later, his breath hot on her throat. "Now that you remember who you really are."

She turned in his arms, nuzzling his jaw. "I'm fond of Jane now."

He chuckled, sliding his hand over the curve of her hip. "What a coincidence," he murmured. "So am I."

\* \* \* \* \*

*Turn the page for a sneak preview of*
**AFTERSHOCK,** *a new anthology*
*featuring* New York Times *bestselling author*
*Sharon Sala.*

*Available October 2008.*

n o c t u r n e ™

*Dramatic and sensual tales of paranormal romance.*

# *Chapter 1*

Nicole Masters was sitting cross-legged on her sofa while a cold autumn rain peppered the windows of her fourth-floor apartment. She was poking at the ice cream in her bowl and trying not to be in a mood.

Six weeks ago, a simple trip to her neighborhood pharmacy had turned into a nightmare. She'd walked into the middle of a robbery. She never even saw the man who shot her in the head and left her for dead. She'd survived, but some of her senses had not. She was dealing with short-term memory loss and a tendency to stagger. Even though she'd been told the problems were most likely temporary, she waged a daily battle with depression.

Her parents had been killed in a car wreck when she was

twenty-one. And except for a few friends—and most recently her boyfriend, Dominic Tucci, who lived in the apartment right above hers, she was alone. Her doctor kept reminding her that she should be grateful to be alive, and on one level she knew he was right. But he wasn't living in her shoes.

If she'd been anywhere else but at that pharmacy when the robbery happened, she wouldn't have died twice on the way to the hospital. Instead of being grateful that she'd survived, she couldn't stop thinking of what she'd lost.

But that wasn't the end of her troubles. On top of everything else, something strange was happening inside her head. She'd begun to hear odd things: sounds, not voices—at least, she didn't think it was voices. It was more like the distant noise of rapids—a rush of wind and water inside her head that, when it came, blocked out everything around her. It didn't happen often, but when it did, it was frightening, and it was driving her crazy.

The blank moments, which was what she called them, even had a rhythm. First there came that sound, then a cold sweat, then panic with no reason. Part of her feared it was the beginning of an emotional breakdown. And part of her feared it wasn't—that it was going to turn out to be a permanent souvenir of her resurrection.

Frustrated with herself and the situation as it stood, she upped the sound on the TV remote. But instead of *Wheel of Fortune,* an announcer broke in with a special bulletin.

"This just in. Police are on the scene of a kidnapping that occurred only hours ago at The Dakota. Molly Dane, the six-year-old daughter of one of Hollywood's blockbuster stars, Lyla Dane, was taken by force from the family apartment. At this time they have yet to receive a ransom demand. The house-keeper was seriously injured during the abduction, and is, at the present time, in surgery. Police are hoping to be able to talk to her once she regains consciousness. In the meantime, we are going now to a press conference with Lyla Dane."

Horrified, Nicole stilled as the cameras went live to where the actress was speaking before a bank of microphones. The shock and terror in Lyla Dane's voice were physically painful to watch. But even though Nicole kept upping the volume, the sound continued to fade.

Just when she was beginning to think something was wrong with her set, the broadcast suddenly switched from the Dane press conference to what appeared to be footage of the kidnapping, beginning with footage from inside the apartment.

When the front door suddenly flew back against the wall and four men rushed in, Nicole gasped. Horrified, she quickly realized that this must have been caught on a security camera inside the Dane apartment.

As Nicole continued to watch, a small Asian woman, who she guessed was the maid, rushed forward in an effort to keep them out. When one of the men hit her in the face with his gun, Nicole moaned. The violence was too reminiscent of what she'd lived through. Sick to her stomach, she fisted her hands against her belly, wishing it was over, but unable to tear her gaze away.

When the maid dropped to the carpet, the same man followed with a vicious kick to the little woman's midsection that lifted her off the floor.

"Oh, my God," Nicole said. When blood began to pool beneath the maid's head, she started to cry.

As the tape played on, the four men split up in different directions. The camera caught one running down a long marble hallway, then disappearing into a room. Moments later he reappeared, carrying a little girl, who Nicole assumed was Molly Dane. The child was wearing a pair of red pants and a white turtleneck sweater, and her hair was partially blocking her abductor's face as he carried her down the hall. She was kicking and screaming in his arms, and when he slapped her, it elicited an agonized scream that brought the other three running. Nicole watched in horror as one of them ran up and put his hand over Molly's face. Seconds later, she went limp.

One moment they were in the foyer, then they were gone.

Nicole jumped to her feet, then staggered drunkenly. The bowl of ice cream she'd absentmindedly placed in her lap shattered at her feet, splattering glass and melting ice cream everywhere.

The picture on the screen abruptly switched from the kidnapping to what Nicole assumed was a rerun of Lyla Dane's plea for her daughter's safe return, but she was numb.

Before she could think what to do next, the doorbell rang. Startled by the unexpected sound, she shakily swiped at the tears and took a step forward. She didn't feel the glass shards piercing her feet until she took the second step. At that point, sharp pains shot through her foot. She gasped, then looked down in confusion. Her legs looked as if she'd been running through mud, and she was standing in broken glass and ice cream, while a thin ribbon of blood seeped out from beneath her toes.

"Oh, no," Nicole mumbled, then stifled a second moan of pain.

The doorbell rang again. She shivered, then clutched her head in confusion.

"Just a minute!" she yelled, then tried to sidestep the rest of the debris as she hobbled to the door.

When she looked through the peephole in the door, she didn't know whether to be relieved or regretful.

It was Dominic, and as usual, she was a mess.

Nicole smiled a little self-consciously as she opened the door to let him in. "I just don't know what's happening to me. I think I'm losing my mind."

"Hey, don't talk about my woman like that."

Nicole rode the surge of delight his words brought. "So I'm still your woman?"

Dominic lowered his head.

Their lips met.

The kiss proceeded.

Slowly.

Thoroughly.

\* \* \* \* \*

*Be sure to look for the*
**AFTERSHOCK** *anthology next month, as*
*well as other exciting paranormal stories*
*from Silhouette Nocturne.*
*Available in October wherever books are sold.*

# nocturne™

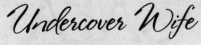

# REQUEST YOUR FREE BOOKS!

## 2 FREE NOVELS
## PLUS 2
## FREE GIFTS!

HARLEQUIN®

## INTRIGUE®

### Breathtaking Romantic Suspense

**YES!** Please send me 2 FREE Harlequin Intrigue® novels and my 2 FREE gifts (gifts are worth about $10). After receiving them, if I don't wish to receive any more books, I can return the shipping statement marked "cancel." If I don't cancel, I will receive 6 brand-new novels every month and be billed just $4.24 per book in the U.S. or $4.99 per book in Canada, plus 25¢ shipping and handling per book and applicable taxes, if any*. That's a savings of close to 15% off the cover price! I understand that accepting the 2 free books and gifts places me under no obligation to buy anything. I can always return a shipment and cancel at any time. Even if I never buy another book from Harlequin, the two free books and gifts are mine to keep forever.

182 HDN EEZ7   382 HDN EEZK

| Name | (PLEASE PRINT) | |
|------|------|------|
| Address | | Apt. # |
| City | State/Prov. | Zip/Postal Code |

Signature (if under 18, a parent or guardian must sign)

Mail to the **Harlequin Reader Service:**
**IN U.S.A.:** P.O. Box 1867, Buffalo, NY 14240-1867
**IN CANADA:** P.O. Box 609, Fort Erie, Ontario L2A 5X3

Not valid to current subscribers of Harlequin Intrigue books.

**Want to try two free books from another line?**
**Call 1-800-873-8635 or visit www.morefreebooks.com.**

\* Terms and prices subject to change without notice. N.Y. residents add applicable sales tax. Canadian residents will be charged applicable provincial taxes and GST. Offer not valid in Quebec. This offer is limited to one order per household. All orders subject to approval. Credit or debit balances in a customer's account(s) may be offset by any other outstanding balance owed by or to the customer. Please allow 4 to 6 weeks for delivery. Offer available while quantities last.

**Your Privacy:** Harlequin is committed to protecting your privacy. Our Privacy Policy is available online at www.eHarlequin.com or upon request from the Reader Service. From time to time we make our lists of customers available to reputable third parties who may have a product or service of interest to you. If you would prefer we not share your name and address, please check here.

HI08R

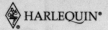
**HARLEQUIN®**

# INTRIGUE®

## COMING NEXT MONTH

### #1089 CHRISTMAS SPIRIT by Rebecca York
*A Holiday Mystery at Jenkins Cove*
Some say old ghosts haunt Jenkins Cove, but not writer Michael Bryant. Can Chelsea Caldwell change his mind—or will ghosts of Christmas past drag the young couple to their doom?

### #1090 PRIVATE S.W.A.T. TAKEOVER by Julie Miller
*The Precinct: Brotherhood of the Badge*
Veterinarian Liza Parrish was nobody special—until she witnessed the murder of KCPD's deputy commissioner. Now she had the city's finest at her disposal, but only needed their bravest, Holden Kincaid, to keep her from harm.

### #1091 SECURITY BLANKET by Delores Fossen
*Texas Paternity*
Quinn "Lucky" Bacelli thought saving Marin Sheppard would be the end of their dalliance. But then she asked him for protection from her domineering parents. And to pretend to be the father of her infant son....

### #1092 MOTIVE: SECRET BABY by Debra Webb
*The Curse of Raven's Cliff*
Someone had taken Camille Wells's baby. It was now up to recluse Nicholas Sterling III to help the woman he once loved and right his past wrongs if he was to save the town from the brink of disaster.

### #1093 MANHUNT IN THE WILD WEST by Jessica Andersen
*Bear Claw Creek Crime Lab*
Federal agent Jonah Fairfax was in over his head, maintaining his cover in a Supermax prison. But when some escapees abducted Chelsea Swan, Jonah was ready to show his true colors in order to save the medical examiner's life.

### #1094 BEAUTIFUL STRANGER by Kerry Connor
Doctor Josh Bennett couldn't deny a woman in distress. Now he had to help Claire Preston uncover the secrets of her past before a hired killer put them both down for good.

www.eHarlequin.com

HICNM0908